Born in the mid-West in 1949, Keith Heller for many years taught English Literature, most recently at a Californian university. Together with his wife and daughter he lived abroad for seven years, three of which were spent in Madrid. He also lived in Japan and Argentina. A published poet, he is the author of the highly-acclaimed, bestselling literary novel, SNOW ON THE MOON. MAN'S STORM is the first in his unusual trio of crime novels, following the career of George Man, a parish watchman in eighteenth-century London. Now retired from university teaching, Keith Heller lives in California where he writes full time.

MAN'S STORM

A Story of

London's Parish Watch, 1703

Keith Heller

HEADLINE

First published in 1985
by WILLIAM COLLINS SONS & CO

This edition first published in 1997
by HEADLINE BOOK PUBLISHING

First published in paperback in 1998
by HEADLINE BOOK PUBLISHING

10 9 8 7 6 5 4 3 2 1

ISBN 0 7472 5684 5

Printed in England by
Clays Ltd, St Ives plc

HEADLINE BOOK PUBLISHING
A division of Hodder Headline PLC
338 Euston Road
London NW1 3BH

One would think the hectoring, the storming, the sullen, and all the different species and subordinations of the angry should be cured, by knowing they live only as pardoned men, and how pityful is the condition of being only suffered?

Richard Steele, *The Spectator*, No. 438
Wednesday, 23 July 1712

AUTHOR'S NOTE

The quotations introducing each chapter are taken from Daniel Defoe's *The Storm: Or, A Collection of the Most Remarkable Casualties and Disasters Which Happen'd in the Late Dreadful Tempest, Both by Sea and Land* (1704).

Part One

Chapter 1

*It had blown exceeding hard, as I have already observed,
for about fourteen days past; and that so hard, that we
thought it terrible weather: . . . and the nearer it came to
the fatal 26th of November, the tempestuousness of the
weather encreased.*

The City of Westminster felt it first, the dark growing from the
south-west of the wind that for two weeks and more had been
loosening the glass in their upper windows and worrying the
wooden slats in their shutters, shuffling the tiles across their
roofs and shifting the bricks in the chimneys with a low grinding
noise that stopped conversations and made the people stare
breathlessly at the ceilings. In the streets, most of them had
grown used to walking with their heads bowed down, one hand
on their hats and the other holding the wings of their coats
together. The hawkers had learned to lean their weight more
heavily on their carts, while the beggars all positioned
themselves downwind to catch up any windblown treasure. Only
the boys seemed in their element, sailing up the streets with
their jackets held open, carelessly ricocheting from one offended
bystander to the next, clearing in easy leaps the broad yellowish
pools of steaming dung and urine.

Yet today, as the afternoon darkened towards evening, even

the boys wrapped their jackets about them and headed for home. The wind was deepening with a distant hollow roar that brought shapeless clouds from over Tothill Fields and brought the shopkeepers to a standstill before their doors, their hands on their hips and their faces turned frowning towards the moving sky. It was a Friday, and most of them wanted to stay open at least until ten and then prepare for the week's last working day. But the crowds were thinning so, and the wind was sending such a blow of debris through the streets, that some started to wonder if it might not be better to shut their glass up early and tight and make a day of it. A penny was a penny, yet it seemed better to lose a little than to lose all.

The shops in the wider, more open streets began to close up first; but even in the narrower lanes and alleys, where the air was usually close and still, the men gathered together and spoke in strained voices. There seemed to be no protection from this wind, no shelter. Today, the eastern, leeward sides of the buildings seemed to feel the force of the gale even more than the windward, as the storm became trapped in corners and twisted back upon itself. In closed alleys, strips of paper and cloth could be seen spiralling in mid-air for minutes at a time; and near the top of King Street, a blind beggar clutching a straw basket half-filled with coins thought himself suddenly bowled over by a gang of rough hands. He struck out and cursed, and a passing boy called him mad.

The south and south-west sections of the city felt the brute force of the wind as it ran in unchecked from the open fields. Among the jostled, overhanging houses in and around the Sanctuaries, the eddies of wind were unpredictable and slow to die. They persisted through even the occasional lulls in the wind overhead and flustered the few walkers who still dared to be abroad. And some of the people swore darkly that there was worse to come.

The woman who stood in the doorway of the ironmonger's shop in Green's Alley looked out into the wind without blinking. She may have squinted a little, as she tried to see first up, then down the length of the deserted street; but this part of the alley, here just below the bend, always caught and trapped the darkness as it did the wind, becoming lightless long before the sky blackened. Now it was past seven, and the heavy clouds forced a dense shadow to fill the street. No householder in this area ever thought to hang out a light on the calmest of nights. And tonight only a few of the houses showed cracks of wavering light through fastened shutters. Even the vague haze that spread outward from the single coffee-house farther up the street seemed weaker than usual, as if the wildness of the wind could affect even the light.

A single candle at the rear of the ironmonger's shop outlined the woman's sharp-angled body. She was of medium height, with a skeleton that seemed to have no real weight on it. The shoulders spiked upward; the elbows made a rough triangle with the head. Her hips were the hips of a boy, but without the boy's lithe strength. They could never be the hips of a woman who had given birth. Even in shadow, the whole body looked dry, brittle. From across the street, it was impossible to tell what expression was on the face. Most probably, none.

She glanced up briefly at the sky, then into the dark street, turned and shut the door. The window was unshuttered, the door unlocked; the ironmonger's shop was still open for business.

The hand-printed sign in the lower right-hand corner of the window, unreadable in the night, read: 'No Trust Upon Retail.'

Through the window, the woman's shadow could be seen

slowly flickering from one side of the room to the other. She would not be pacing with worry – neither for the storm nor for the fact that she was alone in the shop. She would be looking over the merchandise, rearranging things needlessly, fiddling. It was a habit with her. The harnesses and spurs never hung quite straight enough for her, the buckets never stood stacked quite high enough, the scythes and the spades always leaned too messily in a corner. Bad for custom, the iron rods thrust out to bark the shin, the rusty hooks reaching up to snag the ladies' skirts. Not that any effort or frustration on her part could ever make much difference: the ironware seemed to have the power to disorganize itself by night, and in the morning the shop would be another impenetrable maze of points and edges. And the few people who might come in to look or buy would be obliged to stumble and grope from front to back, cursing or mumbling, making strained apologies for the spilled cask of hinges and catching the spade just before it fell.

And the darkness of the place, always darker inside than out, whatever the time or the weather. Even now, the unlit street seemed by contrast a somewhat paler shade of black. It was as if the shop's haphazard collection of old and stained iron attracted and concentrated all the darker colours: shadows clung naturally at the base of upended hammers, a blue-black ink settled along the blades, sombre purple sank to the bottoms of shallow pails. By day, the room was a cave, so that people stepping in from the street were forced to stand for a moment, blind and helpless. At night, the shop was a study in darkness, the iron resting dense and rooted like formations of wet rocks at the shore. The sharp details of nails and spikes disappeared and were replaced by bulk and weight. A score of candles could never have lightened the place; and the woman never allowed more than one.

She would be in there now, feeling her way about, complaining that all the work was hers to do, and then making more work to be done.

The wind kept on. A mass of air that felt wider than the street bulged its way northwards. Its cold cut the face. A man moved before it, running faster than he could run. A few minutes later, a group of three men struggled down the street. They stopped for a moment before the ironmonger's shop with their heads close together, then hurried on. The meowing of a cat slipped by.

The first-floor window of the house was dark, but a faint colourless glow lay somewhere behind it. That would be the widow in the back room, still sitting up over her sewing, tightening her stitches with a half-smile. She would stay up even after she had laid her needle aside, leaning back in her chair with her eyes fixed on the candle, thinking and planning. She never came down into the shop after dark, and she seldom went out.

The other lodger, the Reverend, would not be back until late. Tonight, he would most likely be fuddled with drink and come weaving along, wholly oblivious of the flying dangers, lost in admiration for the way the wind tore at the clouds. A harmless enough man, of no threat to anyone.

At eight, the shadow of the woman in the shop stopped moving about. She had a small stool behind the counter in the back where she liked to sit and review the day's business. She would move the candle close to the frayed black-leather book and drop her head almost to the page, tracing her finger under the numbers and soundlessly moving her lips. Sometimes a stray hair would drift into the flame and burn and curl with a musky singed smell. She never noticed.

She would never put up the shutters until nine. The storm

meant nothing to her. Perhaps a late walker might be in need of something in a hurry, and she could ask a dearer price. Or someone in the neighbourhood might want an extra rod to brace his door against the wind. Or her husband might return early from his nightly scavenging with something of value: something heavy or new, or something that had been blown far enough away from its owner to be had without dealing or asking. This could be a night of windfall for her, though she would expect her husband only to shelter himself in some costly coffee-house all the evening. She never trusted him to keep to business. In her eyes, he was barely half a man.

A sudden crash of dislodged pantiles shook the street. Something large and wooden was rolled with a monotonous rumble up Green's Alley and round the bend. The wind was maddening in its regularity: it never stopped, it never failed to find its way into the narrowest recess between buildings and tug at whoever was cowering there. It was everywhere at once, pressing itself against a man's chest until he felt that he must break free.

The thick, smeared window-glass of the ironmonger's shop showed the woman nodding over her ledger, the candle burning low but steadily. From a distance, she appeared to be framed in a dark picture. The heavy surrounding clutter of iron seemed to grow out of the rain-soaked wood of the window, and the woman sat buried at the centre, a stack of spade-handles leaning towards her. Occasionally, she jerked her head up and looked about her and at the window; but even in full daylight the glass made a grey blur of the traffic passing in the street, and now the small casements looked empty. The card in the lower corner was a vague rounded smudge that seemed to move slightly in the wind.

At nine o'clock the woman stirred herself awake and put her

book behind the low counter. She stood up and swivelled her head and massaged her neck. The cheap cotton of her dress lay flat across her chest. She looked with boredom about the shop, seemed to listen for a moment to the straining of the house in the wind, and raised her face to the ceiling. She smiled – secretly, comfortably. Her hands moved slowly up her hips, across her belly and breasts to her throat, where they seemed to tremble. Then she moved out of the candle's light.

Now, as every night, she would go into the tiny back room where the shutters, the candles and a few pieces of broken or bent iron were kept. She did not need the light; she knew by touch where the hardwood shutters stood leaning against the back wall. She took longer than was necessary in getting them out; but they were heavy and cumbersome, and the hinges often caught in the piles of objects on the floor.

On the counter, the candle wavered and almost went out.

When she came back into the main room, struggling with the awkwardness of the shutters, she could feel her anger and impatience rising. Why was he not at home to help her in this work? Why did he have to go out each night, when he always brought in so little? Her arms were strong, stronger than his; but it would be hard to set the shutters right in the wind. A shattered glass now would be a senseless expense. She consoled herself with the thought that, if she hurried, her lodger upstairs might still be awake and ready for conversation.

She stopped suddenly at the end of the counter and set the bottoms of the shutters on the floor. She had heard nothing more than the ceaseless wind, seen nothing more than the usual darkness. Yet something in the shop seemed different somehow, something had changed since she had gone into the back room.

She sniffed. That was it. A draught of cold, fresh air. The front door had been opened and closed.

For a moment, the skin on her face tightened and she felt a sick looseness in her bowels. She surveyed the room quickly, but could see no figure or shadow that did not belong. The room lay still and dark; the mass of iron seemed to anchor the shop to the earth, and she could hear nothing moving. Only the wind.

Then a dull noise of something falling at the side of the shop near the spades, and she began to pant like an animal. There, behind some casks of chains, a rounded shadow shifted about on the floor. It looked like a great dog; but then how could a dog have shut the door? She instinctively took up the shutters and clasped them in her arms before her. She yearned to run upstairs to the safety of the bedrooms, to the widow, but she could not move. Briefly, she thought of her husband, but she knew he would be of no use to her now.

The figure on the floor reared up on its haunches, its narrow back still turned towards her, and she became again the sensible woman of business. It was a customer, rummaging about in this infernal mess in search of something which he probably needed at once. It was foolish of her not to have thought of it before. She felt ashamed of her fears. What reason had she to be uneasy? Here was the final chapman of the day, the one she had been waiting for. There could be good business here.

Forgetting that she still held the shutters, she stepped forward until she stood within a few feet of the hunched-over figure. She could now see the common black coat, but she could not tell if the customer were a man or a woman. No matter. Trade was trade.

She lowered the shutters and politely cleared her throat.

''Evening. Was there something?'

Quickly, in a single motion, the customer stood erect and spun about. The long spade swung in a tight arc and struck her

10

with terrific force, the sharp blade entering her head just above the right ear. She felt no pain, only the massive weight of the blow. She heard a distant rushing of air, felt as if a huge wind were lifting her, pushing her over, she could not stand. The weight of her body tilted the shutters, something she could not resist was turning her and she was falling. She had wet herself. The candle seemed to have gone out.

She was standing again behind the customer.

''Evening. Was there something?'

The sound of the spade again, slicing through the air. The blow.

She was standing again behind the customer.

''Evening. Was there something?'

The force of the blow shot through her entire body and twitched her feet on the rough floor.

She was standing, again and again.

''Evening . . . 'Evening . . .'

Each repeated blow reverberated into a separate part of her body: the arms, the stomach, the groin. She heard a pounding, the sound of a hammer in wet sand, far away.

Her hands lay resting quietly upon the floor. The fingers clawed convulsively, then were still.

She had made no sound, dying. A low ticking, as of a clicking tongue, sounded through the dark ironmonger's shop, but it was lost in the greater noise of the wind beating upon the roof.

The coaching-inn at Tilbury was closed on account of the storm. Yet in the front parlour, before a loud fire, two people – a man and a young girl – stood talking with their coats on.

Raymond Chambers was a calm, almost inert man with the squinting face of those used to driving fast into a sharp wind and brick-like hands that would never feel the lash of leather or rain. He had a broad, spatulate nose that smiled when he did, which was most of the time. He was a good man, and his goodness was strengthened by his never bothering to consider the worth of his actions. He also had the distracting habit of hacking and spitting, indoors and out, in the middle of nearly every wandering sentence.

'Now as I was after telling ye, Missy, a finer flying-coach'n mine's nary to be landed in Tilbury Town this time a-clock, as you yourself knows from spending most o' this day in trying to find one to borrow. And my horses got their hearts in them, they do. And no man knows the run better'n me, light or dark. But, as I say, only as far as Spitalfields: I ain't got the face for driving the town. Now, as to the time—' here a neat glob was flung to the floor between them – 'London's no long ride in day or night. In clear air, we could see it by tomorrow day easy. But this night we're to be staring up into something more'n half a storm, if my knuckles don't lie, and I can't answer for the health of the roads, what with the trees fallen crost it and the wet drove into it so, not to speak to a lady like yourself of the high-pads as might be along of it. This is their weather, Missy, fine biting weather. Why it's got to be tomorrow's past me anyways. You might well stand a day or three and then fly in with your hat in your lap. And a last thing, Miss Castleton—' another wet flake landed with the slap of a rag, this time somewhat closer to the girl – 'is that I know your father as well as myself, and a fairer man there never was what lost his position from behind him as he done. It's none o' his sin that them tile-works fell the way they did: that's to be laid to them in London what spend their days in the Numans 'stead o' at their business. But he's a good one, as any can tell, and you're his oldest girl, though still some short of full-growed, to my mind, and I'm thinking it needs his nod for you to be taking yourself off alone this way. I think finely of you, Daughter, but I won't be stirring myself a yard without that good man's approval.' The full stop was provided by a huge ball of phlegm, lobbed expertly and with some pride in the execution, precisely between the toes of the girl's shoes.

Pamela Castleton stepped back an inch and moved her right glove from hand to hand. She was a small girl, but not delicate. Her figure was strong and full, and she had a clear and simple face – pretty and innocent, not yet beautiful. She was eighteen, with all the half-knowledge and the scared fearlessness of the young. She was running away from her father's house. She knew what she was doing.

She worried the glove back and forth and spoke in a strained, excited tone. Her voice squeaked a little.

'I have given you, Mr Chambers, as much as is the expected fee for your conducting me into London. And a bit more, as you well know. Should it still not prove to be enough—'

The man interrupted her, speaking softly.

'The money's naught to me, Missy. You've heard my objections.'

The girl flushed. She had known Raymond Chambers since her childhood; he was a kind and gentle man. She did not want to argue with him, lie to him.

'I do not wish, Sir, to ask too much of you or of your horses. I, too, should much rather travel under more benign conditions. I had not expected this weather to worsen so, nor so terrifically, else I had engaged your services much earlier in the week.'

She took a step forward and held her chin up high.

'But that I mean to set forth tonight and that I must arrive in London no later than tomorrow evening are certain, and I will not be put off. Tomorrow is the twenty-seventh of the month and it is of the greatest importance to me that I be in the city on that day.' Here her voice faltered, and she looked quickly down at the floor. 'I – I cannot tell you, Sir, what it means to me to do this. I have waited for this past year for this one day to come. I must not miss it now. I must be free to do this thing, Mr Chambers.'

The man regarded her kindly and remained silent. He had known Miss Pamela all her life; she had played often enough with his own Molly. She was a good girl, serious and respectful. Yet in the past year he thought he had noticed some change come over her – a wistfulness, a far-off look in her face as she walked the few streets of Tilbury. His Molly had seen it, too, but she swore she did not know the cause. Now, he wondered if his own daughter might not know more than she was telling him.

He turned and sailed a spreading crab that fell hissing into the fire a full five feet away.

'And you know London, don't you, Miss? Been there afore now, ain't you?'

The girl grew more animated.

'Yes, of course, a good number of times. You need have no caution towards me on that point. I have a number of friends in both London and Westminster who will provide for me. I shall not be alone, and my lodgings are already secured.'

Nodding, the man moved thoughtfully towards the fire. He stared into it, moodily stroking his unshaven chin. The horses in the attached stables were restless and cold; the wind could be heard furiously shaking the trees. A branch broke with a long crack that sounded curiously like a human voice.

Raymond Chambers spat once more into the heart of the fire and briskly turned back to the girl.

'Well then, I'm thinking we'll be for trying it. I'll ready the horses, Missy, and come to call you when they're set.' As he

neared the door, he added over his shoulder: 'And we'll just
stop for a breath along the way at your father's, just to listen
for his blessing on it.'

'No!'

The girl had been about to put on her glove, as the man had
crossed the room towards the door. Now she ran up to him,
frantically twisting her glove, almost crying.

'No, please, I beg of you, we must not do that!' She could
not meet his eyes. 'It – it is – something that concerns my father
himself that takes me this night to London. Something that
touches him deeply.' She exhaled unevenly, hiccuping. 'You
must know, then, that I go to London on his behalf, to try to
beg a respite from his creditors or some kind of aid from Mr
Defoe himself. I had thought perhaps that a young girl might
be able somehow to move their compassion; but if my father
should hear of my going, his shame would not allow it.'

She raised her head to look at the driver. She's fair scared,
he thought, but true as a line. He admired her courage and
hoped to see the same someday in his Molly. Yet he knew the
girl was lying.

He smiled grimly to himself and turned to go.

The coach had lurched and swayed past the stripped roof of
the Dissenters' meeting-house and past the bleak ruins of the
abandoned brick-and-tile factory, before Pamela Castleton had
to force her head out of the side of the coach and vomit on to
the pitching road. She sat back then, feeling somewhat better,
and closed her eyes, thinking: Tomorrow, tomorrow all will be
well, tomorrow . . .

Raymond Chambers urged his team onward into the wind
and the dark, a steady stream of spit trailing behind him like a
banner.

Chapter 2

On Friday morning, it continued to blow exceeding hard,
but not so as that it gave any apprehensions of danger
within doors; towards night it encreased: . . .

John Manneux was a man who worried too much. He knew it,
and it worried him. It showed in his round, florid face. Some of
his customers argued that they could judge the quality of the
day's wines simply by gauging the redness of his cheeks and
counting the number of grooves between his overhanging
eyebrows. He had also a ruined, rasping voice that seemed to
have been born to complain.

It was the business that worried him most. If the shop were
too full, then perhaps his stock would give out or his service
would be too slow. If the shop were not full enough, then it
must be the fault of his wines or his help that kept the people
away. It was a good enough house, to be sure. The Carved
Balcony had stood in Pall Mall since the year of the Great
Fire, and it had been selling wines for almost twenty years,
since the time of old Henry Rugeley. But John Manneux himself
had only had the business for a year now, and he was anxious
about making a good beginning.

He stood now at the back of the shop, surveying his customers
or looking through the leaded-glass windows at the traffic

passing in the Mall, some of it curving off to the right into St Alban's Street. There were far fewer people, both in the shop and in the street, than he would normally have expected for a Friday afternoon. It was the wind that was keeping them from going too far abroad, that much was a certainty. Today his customers could talk of nothing else but the storm which they felt was about to descend upon Westminster, a monster of a storm that would level the buildings on top of the people and spoil the city's goods both in the warehouses and in the ships that were riding crowded together in the Thames. He felt little concern about his own house: The Carved Balcony was stout enough to stand for another century at the least. But how long could he keep it, if the business failed to thrive better? Now, the room was only half full, and he expected that most of these few would want to run home early, before dark. No sane man would wish to be out in the streets tonight.

John Manneux scanned the room again, still worrying, until finally he was looking at a young man who was sitting alone near the window. He was a sturdy-looking man, no more than five-and-twenty years of age, with a high broad forehead that gave him a stern expression that did not match well with the gentleness of the rest of his features. One of his wide strong hands held a long pipe, and the blue fog of the smoke hung lazily about his head. He wore a soiled greatcoat with the uneasiness of a young man who has come to a public place and feels too conscious of the way the older men have watched him walk in. He was just now draining his second glass of wine and signalling diffidently for a third.

John Manneux decided suddenly to take the bottle over to the watchman himself. Young George Man had been one of his earliest and most frequent customers; evidently, he had been in the habit of stopping in at The Carved Balcony at least once a day even before Manneux took the place over. That the proprietor had often to extend a week's credit to the watchman was one of the few things that Manneux did not worry about. He trusted George Man.

He poured until the wine slopped over the rim of the glass.

'Here's another for you, George, my lad, that'll keep your bowels well-blowed!'

The vintner reviewed the shop critically, as he lowered himself on to a low stool across from the watchman.

'Hardly half a crew in here most of the day. And these'll be flown with the sun, if I study them correctly.'

He did not speak in anger, but in worry. Both men glanced at the various groups scattered about the room. At one table, a trio of finely dressed, extravagantly wigged gentlemen were talking with their heads brought to a point over the table. Occasionally, one or another of them would shout the name 'Anne', and then all would drink the new Queen's health. At a table near the back of the shop, five prosperous countrymen were playing half-heartedly at skittles; every minute, they stopped the play to raise their heads in unison and listen to the wind as it came hurtling out of the Park and over the house. The few remaining customers were distributed singly or in pairs about the shop – some talking, some reading the *Daily Courant*, one almost sleeping. The room was too quiet for an afternoon; the rushing of the wind outside seemed to dampen all sounds.

John Manneux looked thoughtfully across the table at the watchman. He had noticed the bruises on the young man's face and his careful way of walking – as if he suffered from a painful hernia – when he had first come in. Now, close up, he could see that the watchman had been badly beaten. The nose was swollen, the lips split, and the skin round the eyes was mottled and puffy.

''Pears to me, son, that this wind's come up against you

some already, by the look of you.'

George Man grinned widely, then winced and tenderly touched the side of his mouth.

'If 'twere the wind only, Mr Manneux, I would hardly be carrying such deep patches about with me now.'

'How did you come to buy them, then?'

The watchman tasted his wine and tapped out his pipe on the edge of the stained table. He spoke with embarrassment.

'Last night it was, as I took a turn in Sea Alley. A devil's dozen of them that style themselves Hawcubites. They were against me before I knew which way to turn. Thereafter, they spent a few minutes of their time introducing me to their shoes and their buckles. I'd had one or two of them down with my staff, but then they closed up ranks and I went under. I should have kept them at the staff's length. It is hardly to my praise as a watchman.'

The vintner studied the young man's powerful hands and the solid build of his arms and shoulders.

'Aye,' he said softly, 'it might well take that many – and more. But listen, boy, you might fair have been killed then, as old Dick Adams was two or three year past, who measured his full length beneath just such hands as those.'

'Nay, these things come and then pass on. And an inch in a miss is as good as an ell.' The watchman looked down at his glass of wine, speaking more to himself. 'Not but that I let it come too close to me, though, and all for my own imperfect watchfulness.'

The proprietor noticed the young man's shame and sought to cover it with his usual bluster.

'Close, you say? Why, boy, 'twas at least that! As close as lies the good Lord's curse to a thin whore's arse, to my way of judging!' He reached across the table and clapped Man on the shoulder – and saw him wince again.

The door opened and the wind filled the room. A few angry shouts closed it.

'But truth, George, why not give this low work the quick go-by once for ever? 'Tis no sort of thing for a young buck of the first head like yourself. This is work for them that has to eat their meat with a spoon. You ought to give yourself to some steadier work that has something in it waiting for you past the morrow.'

The watchman smiled and slowly nodded his head.

'You speak my mother's own words now, Sir. She is ever at me to give this work over and come to join her at the brewery. She says as how there's more than enough work for the two of us.'

''Tis thriving, then? Your mother has driven it well since your father's going.'

'Aye, never better than these eight years.' He gave a short, barking laugh. 'Good Tetty's on to sixty-four this year, and she works the men well into the next month. This last spring, when the cellar took in three to four foot of water, it was Tetty herself who punted a raft across the pool to the casks. She is quite such a mixture, is Tetty. In some manner, she holds to the past – would never wash a thread of clothes in soap, but still bucks them with the lees of ash and hog's dung. Yet she swears 'tis no disgrace for a woman to pick up her man's work where he leaves it off – especially a widow like herself – and that there be many women in the brewing trade these times. She calls it long, honest work –' his voice dropped – 'which is a mortal sight more than she says of the watching.'

The vintner took another look round the shop, then narrowed his eyes at Man.

'And how long is it now you've been at the watch? Six year, ain't it?'

'No, eight.' A pained look crossed the young man's face as he said this, as if it called back an unhappy memory.

George Man brought out a bulging leather pouch of tobacco and began to fill his pipe. The proprietor motioned a boy to bring a lit straw from the fire, then he sat forward with his short arms crossed upon the table, intently watching his companion. He was considering those qualities which he had come to admire in the young watchman: courage, seriousness, a steadiness that he did not often see nowadays in men so young. He found himself thinking about his business.

'Not been at it steady, though, have you?'

'No, no. What man could be? I tried other work, but I could never make a hand of it. Even returned to the brewery for times; but Tetty values her independence, for all she says. So I hire myself out to the needful constable or for a week or a month to guard some house or shop or take the place of one who has no time or wish to serve.'

'That last's not the law, George.'

'But common enough. And there's talk of a change there soon.'

'And what was it started you at the first?'

The watchman turned to stare out into the street and pulled slowly at his pipe.

'Did you ever know one constable in the City called Innes?'

Manneux nodded. 'I know the name, nothing more.'

'I was his student. He taught me as much of the canters and of their society and language as I know.' The watchman suddenly pointed out the window with the stem of his pipe. 'Look you there, Mr Manneux. See you that man passing?'

The vintner saw a tall man with an iron sword and a flapping hat which was pinned up on one side. He walked alone and as if there were no wind.

'Notice how his doublet is buttoned by intercession only. 'Tis his badge, as mine is my coat and my staff. It tells the town, both friend and foe, that here walks a cheat. And the napper wears his glove hanging, made fast by one finger, and the better cut-purse carries a little white mark in his hat. Mr Innes introduced me into his world and taught me how to run in it. In some ways, his death was harder to me than my own father's.'

The two men were silent for a long moment.

John Manneux was looking carefully at the watchman, trying to understand why such a fine young man should want to throw away his best years. Manneux had seen the watch of Westminster often enough – or, rather, had had to try to find them when they were needed. Most of them spent as many of their working hours as they could curled up asleep within the walls of the warmest and safest watch-house. They were old and fumbling; and when they did go out, they were hardly able to drag themselves from corner to corner. And they could be easily bought by any passing bully with arrogance or with coin. How many times had Manneux himself had to rouse one of their crew out of the lowest gin-cellar and help to carry him to his work? Not that he had had any but the best report of young George Man: but a man, he thought, gets to be known by those he lies with.

The proprietor stroked his flaming cheek.

'I can see, George, your running after the excitement of it as a mere boy; but why do you stay in it still?'

The watchman was about to reply, but stopped himself. Instead, he slowly moved his eyes among the men in the shop. An argument was heating up between two merchants in one corner, balanced by the sound of drunken laughter in another. When he finally spoke, it was in a voice that was hoarse and puzzled.

'I cannot say, Sir, that I am altogether certain of that.'

John Manneux had come to a decision. He leant forward and tapped the table with a hard finger.

'Then heed me now, George, for I have that to say that may be of long value to the both of us. I am alone here in this business, except for my wife, and I know not when – or if – that good dame will gift me with a son to stand ahint me. It's a straight trade and a paying one: don't trust too much to what you see this God-abandoned day. You yourself have sat here often enough to know. To my thinking, 'twould be something for a young one like yourself to build on, and I could well do with another pair of hands round here. I don't care to look for to 'prentice no boy: what I need is another man in the house, and I need him now, not a set of years forward.'

They were interrupted by a short, stocky woman with a face that looked as warm and wholesome as fresh-baked bread. She came up to their table and laid a wet hand on the vintner's shoulder.

'I beg to be excused, John, but you're wanted down to the cellar.'

'Aye, Mrs Manneux, I'm all but there already.'

They both watched her trundle off, and the older man smiled and winked at the younger. He felt in a teasing mood.

'Now there, George-my-son, is what you're standing most in need of – particularly on such a night as we're all facing today – a good and warm, heavy-haunched length of leather that'll lend you a stretch of her garden to take your cover in!' The watchman squirmed in his chair, colouring violently. 'But hold, then, boy! That's true! You've not yet joined the giblets with one, have you? I thought as how you seemed riding a little low in the stones when you stepped in here. Then what's the delay, lad? You surely can't mean to go hiding yourself out at Picket-Hatch for the rest of your days? There's a burning dripper waiting for you there, you know!'

He stood up, relishing Man's discomfort, then bent over him, suddenly serious.

'But listen, George, this talk of tail minds me that there'll be more than bricks and tiles flying the streets tonight. Believe me, the nightcaps will be in full swing. You're to be working where, then?'

'Round the Sanctuaries, as before.'

Manneux resumed his habitual worried expression.

'Aye, then you'll be wanting to be on the look for them Tumblers as have been about down that way these weeks. Me, I don't let my woman out, day or night. What they do to the ladies don't well bear speaking of. And tonight, with this storm abroad, a man can't fair be the same as a man. I'll say you ought to keep as close a watch upon yourself as well, my boy, considering what fell upon you last night.'

As he moved away, he pointed back at the watchman.

'And hold my thought for the trade afore ye, George Man. You've got to look forward to your business.'

He ambled towards the back of the shop, looking worriedly from side to side as he went.

When Man finally stepped out into the street, the wind drove against him with such violence that the bruises on his face began to smart. Bits of dirt, sometimes whole clods, were being hurled through the air. Two men crossed the watchman's path, their talk flung over their shoulders by the wind. Man caught something about the new stacks of chimneys in the still-unfinished part of the Palace and how they must fall in the coming gale.

The watchman started walking, bent over into the wind, still favouring his wounded groin. He was making for the Gate House at the end of Tothill Street to speak to the Constable there about his night's work.

He skirted the Park along its western edge, swaying slightly from the odd surges of air that were carried from over the Canal. He could smell water in the wind. A few birds struggled helplessly through the air. The brim of his hat flapped like wings.

Of the few people who were abroad, the watchman must have been the only one who did not seem to mind the wind. He walked along much as he always did, slowly and methodically. He was thinking about what John Manneux had said, what he had offered. Man knew that the vintner himself was active in some kind of parish office – the watchman had never learned exactly which – during what time he could spare from The Carved Balcony. And the dual career seemed to work well enough for him: Man supposed that he made good use of his public position to attract trade and to make his importing run more smoothly. About that, at least, Man had not yet heard him complain.

The watchman had just reached the middle of Long Ditch, still limping low into the growing wind, when a motley group of young and tattered boys moved straggling out from a side-street. Arranging themselves in a crude half-circle before him, they confronted him with a set speech, their screeching voices keeping somehow in tune with the high rushing of the wind.

'Westminster Black Guard are we, Sir, marching to our winter quarters. Lord bless you, if you should bend to give us a bare penny or a half, amongst us, and you shall hear any of us, if you please, say the Lord's Prayer backwards at speed, swear the compass round as fair as any fish-stall trull, give a new curse to every step in the Monument, call a harlot as many proper names as a lady hath hidden hairs, repeat the names of fresh-murdered babes, tell the ages of ready virgins, cast the fates of secret millers . . .'

They made as if to continue, some of the boys jostling each other with competing indecencies; but Man, affecting a gruff tone, gave them three pennies and ordered them to take themselves off. They ran laughing up the street, the wind fluttering their rags, their bare feet a dirty white in the half-light. One shouted that he knew a gin-stall nearby where the drink could be had both cheap and hot.

The watchman moved on. He was thinking that he had long cherished a boyhood dream of someday having his own shop: of rising early and going down to the shop before dawn, sanding the floor and readying the cups, then opening up to a long day of drinking and smoking and talking – but mostly of observing, of watching the passing of the people, each with his unique way of thinking and living. It would be a calm, settled life, one with none of the usual tedium and sudden dangers that came with the watch. One that he might someday be able to pass on to his own son . . .

Towards the end of Long Ditch, the wind stormed in viciously from the nearby open country and blew up the funnel of the street. Man walked bent almost double. The street was darkening. The shopkeepers worked frantically to tie up their shutters; the few people walking seemed all to be moving before the wind, their legs barely able to catch up with them as they ran and stumbled in a strange, loose-jointed dance. Man saw one proud gentlewoman hurried by in a confused flutter of clothes, chased by a rolling washtub that still swirled a handful of suds round its bottom.

At the junction of Broken Cross, just as Man was about to straighten up in the shelter of a projecting wall, a blurred figure was swung about the corner and thrust roughly into him. It was a young girl, breathless and flushed, panting like a puppy. The tip of a small, pink tongue hung over a slightly swollen lower lip.

Man had caught her in his arms to keep the wind from tumbling her over. Now, as she looked boldly up at him, smiling, she moved her body closer to his. He felt a large firm breast flattened against his chest, its point hardening behind the thin fabric of the dress, and a strong warm leg angled up between his thighs. The girl's hands sought an entrance into his greatcoat as she spoke.

'Well met, Dick! 'Tis a wind on us here to be well out of, to my mind, for both the bull and the cow!'

Her hands worked fast at the crease of his breeches, until Man pushed her gently away, made a quick bow, and walked off almost at a run. His neck and ears burned, and there was a new aching in his walk.

John Manneux had been right about that, at least. The watchman was too much alone.

From across the street, a rough voice shouted out of a dark window.

'Watch, what's a-clock, by the Lor's' grace?'

'Almost on to nine now, Sir!'

'And the climate, Watch, how rides that, eh?'

The watchman spat angrily into the air, as he seemed to hear a nasty chuckle just before the window slammed securely shut.

It had already been a long night for Man, with only a fraction of it behind him. He seemed to have walked a full half of Westminster, and most of it against the wind. He had ranged far beyond the streets assigned to him, partly out of dedication and partly out of curiosity. The streets seemed darker than ever tonight, yet somehow more alive, with the wind's filling them with noise and danger. There were fewer people out, but those few seemed worse than usual – more reckless and excited, almost hysterical, and uncontrollable. Man had felt no shame in turning off Gardiner's Lane to avoid a company of swearing revellers; he could remember too well his stark fear of the night before, as he could still feel the pain. Tonight, he meant to be more careful.

And in all of his walking, from the widest streets to the most obscure alleys, he had yet to see a sign of another watchman.

Constable Burton had predicted as much, when Man had talked with him at the Gate House:

'Thou wert born a fool, George Man, if thou art thinking of exposing thyself in the streets this night. Every mother's wise son shall be hiding himself in the warmest thicket he can find, and our good watch shall be no exception. Think better of thyself, lad, and give thyself a double sleep this night and day. The night-snaps do not need thee, and the rest of the citizens be damned!'

Yet Man had been needed. In King Street, at the lower end, he had found a woman fighting against the wind to close her door. She had been working at it for over an hour, before Man came.

In Duffin's Alley, he had taken up a leather bucket and joined a dozen householders against a blaze that had threatened to engulf a ground-floor grocery. The fire had burned small, but fiercely. From one side, they could not come near it: from the other, they were all but blown into the heart of it. It had taken them nearly an hour to contain the fire that was being constantly fed by the rising wind.

And in Antelope Alley, where Man himself kept lodgings over a tripe-shop, the watchman had noticed a low mound of darker shadow on the step of a dilapidated house without lights. Bending over and training his lanthorn on the step, he had found a homemade wicker basket, covered by a thread-bare pink blanket. To it was pinned a note, horribly spelled and ill-written in charcoal. It was a poem of sorts, of which Man could only make sense of the closing; 'For al that my muther can say, The Pairish must be my father.'

Inside, sleeping as contentedly as if the wind were the rocking hand and the humming voice of a woman, was a very young baby.

It had taken Man some time to make his way back to the Gate House and entrust the basket to the Constable. Such finds did not affect the watchman as deeply as they had during the earlier years of his work. They were so common.

Now, Man was resting for a moment in the upper reaches of Long Ditch, crouching at the side of a barrel, still feeling angry at the smug complacency of the man at the window. The storm howled about the niche where Man was sheltering, filling his ears with a deafening hollowness. The faint light of his lanthorn showed the dust and cinders being hurled through the air like snowflakes.

He had just raised himself to go about his work, when he noticed a light, moving erratically at the head of the street. It was a link-boy, struggling against the wind, coming towards him. Behind the boy, a taller shadow walked more slowly and with more assurance.

Seeing the watchman's lanthorn, the pair swerved from the middle of the street. Man waited for them to come up to him, thinking they would be wanting to get out of the wind.

In the combined light of the two lamps, the watchman looked at a young man about his own age who carried himself in a studied posture of arrogance and impatience. He wore a long sword that caught the light and a well-cut grey coat. Man thought his face looked too fine and effeminate, one that would most likely give way soon to dissipation.

The young man spoke at a point somewhere above the watchman's head.

'I beg you, Watchman, to come at your haste, if you will be so good. There is a matter of the utmost urgency which requires your presence.'

As the link-boy was dispatched with a coin and the two men set out at a fast walk up Long Ditch, the watchman was wondering if it had been only his imagination or if he had heard in the voice a note of uncertainty or shame.

They came in a few minutes to a new and handsome house in Dartmouth Street. It was broad and faced with the most expensive bricks, three storeys high, its five windows looking westward on to the slightly older Park Street and the still-developing square beyond. The front door was huge and gleamed richly in the light of the lanthorn.

Without a word, the young man led the watchman into a front parlour that was so neat and tastefully arranged that Man began to worry about how clean his boots were. He was left alone for a moment, until the young man returned with his father.

Michael Wells was a tall, solid man in his early fifties. He was a sign-painter by trade; and, as Man was to learn later, quite a talented and successful one. He had a booming voice, a jaw like the blade of a shovel, and permanently stained fingers. He seemed the kind of man who could not be hurried and who had never found the slightest reason to doubt himself.

The watchman took an instant liking to him, probably because, as he spoke, the father rested one of his broad, painted hands on Man's shoulder.

The son, Daniel, stood off to one side and never spoke a

word. Man did not much like the way he was examining his greatcoat from frayed collar to mud-splashed hem.

'You will pardon me, Sir, for my calling you away from your hard work in such a brusque manner. The fact of the matter is that my only daughter, returning home late this evening with her brother here, suffered some verbal abuse from a gentleman in the street which I cannot with honour allow to go unanswered. I had thoughts of going to apprehend the fellow myself, but my daughter will not see it. As we know where the bully is stopping, I did not wish to lose much time, but sent my son out in search of one of your company. If I apply to you, Sir, it is because I do not want to lose sight of the man before he is brought to law.'

The son had moved off to one side of the room and was idly toying with an embroidered curtain. He kept his face turned away, but Man could see that his ears were red. The watchman wondered why the young man had been unable to defend his sister.

'And whereabouts did this offence occur, Mr Wells?'

The father's face grew dark and his voice rumbled.

'Outside the Royal Cockpit, at the head of this same street. My son says that the man went directly within.' The sign-painter gripped Man's shoulder hard and thrust his face closer. The watchman caught the smell of a good brandy. 'And that, Sir, is yet another thing of which I have long sued for satisfaction: the rowdiness and the impudence of those gamesters has become unbearable in a decent street.'

The watchman and Daniel Wells had passed by the Cockpit on their way to the house. Even the violence of the storm seemed to have little effect on the successive waves of shouting and argument that had surged out of the windows and the door. And the beggars lounging before it had looked particularly mean and surly.

'Do you know the man's name, Sir?'

'My daughter, as you can well imagine, did not seek to learn it.'

Man turned towards the son.

'Perhaps you, Sir, have seen this man before or know of him?'

Daniel Wells stared at the watchman with a petulance that made his face seem childish.

'I do not, Sir, frequent such entertainments, nor do I number such louts among my acquaintances – as you yourself should know, Sir, were you in a position to know me better.'

In the silence that followed, Man noticed for the first time that the sound of the wind barely penetrated into this house. All that could be heard was a distant hum.

'Then you would not mind walking with me now to the Cockpit to single this man out for me from the crowd? Else you set me to look for the needle in the bottle of hay.'

Into the young man's face came a look that may have been disgust, but the watchman thought it was fear.

'I could not help you, Sir. The darkness prevented me from seeing him closely. Perhaps my sister . . .'

'I'll not have my girl step one foot into that cave of drunken Alsatians! I am shocked at you, boy, for even suggesting such an action!'

The son blushed and looked down at the floor. He started to move out of the room.

'Then I shall fetch her here so that she may give a description of the man to this – gentleman.'

Sarah Wells looked to be about eighteen or nineteen years of age. She was not beautiful, perhaps not even pretty; but Man noticed at once her honest and calm face and the self-confidence in her walk. Simply dressed, she was somewhat heavy in body, but the hands were delicate and the eyes were deep and steady. She spoke in a low, but strong voice, the kind that Man had always admired in those few women who felt perfectly at ease with themselves.

'Really, Father, I do not think we need impose upon this kind gentleman or take his time from him. You feel the offence far more closely than I. No real injury has been done.'

The son had not returned with his sister, and Man at last felt comfortable in the warm parlour with the gruff sign-painter and his friendly daughter.

'Yet the injury, Miss Wells, might have been real, had your brother not been at your side.' Man thought that she seemed grateful to him for saying this. Her brother had probably been more frightened than she. 'If you could describe the man to me, I should be happy to go and deal with him as I see fit.'

Her forehead creased in concentration.

'He is a tall man, somewhat taller than you, Sir. And perhaps a decade older. A rough-looking man, although some others might call him handsome. What I could see of his face in the shadow seemed marked to me, wild, almost bestial. And he limped, I believe, on his left leg, and I think he was what is sometimes called caudge-pawed – that is to say left-handed, is it not?'

Man was surprised at her knowing the term.

'And how did you learn which hand he favours?'

She smiled faintly, and the next words she spoke brought a blush to Man's cheeks and sent her father grumbling to the back of the room.

'I cannot say for certain, Sir, but I believe that a man uses his more favoured hand when he sets himself to open his breeches. Is that not true?'

Man himself had to smile. She spoke not from an assumed

innocence, but with a frankness that seemed to him totally natural.

'But you would not know his name.'

'I am sorry, no. Yet he had two friends who stood somewhat behind him, talking together, and in the wind I thought I heard the name, "Robin". But whether that is this man's name or not, I do not know.'

As Man was taking his leave of the house, the young woman looked at him with what he thought was worry.

'Take care first for yourself, Sir. My pride is not worth your pain.'

The watchman stood alone outside the house, the wind tugging at his coat. He was wishing his face had not looked quite so shamefully battered. He wanted desperately to know exactly what Sarah Wells had thought of him.

The Royal Cockpit was a squat tower of a building, encircled by a series of upended rectangular openings that appeared as sombre machicolations in an ancient battlement. The wind sang through these and carried out a breaking comb of smoke with a mad clamour of screaming voices.

Man had, of course, visited the Cockpit before. Cocking was one of his favourite diversions, and he prided himself on having a good eye for birds. But he enjoyed the feinting and the warring of the gamesters nearly as much as that of the cocks – the absurd arguing over the valour shown in each cock's eye, the hurried betting and the exchange of money, then the frantic urging of the birds in battle, followed by the incredulous dismay of the losers. The pit was a condensation of the city streets through which Man walked almost every night.

He was long used to the wildness of the Cockpit, as wild as Bedlam; but tonight, perhaps because of the wind or the threat of the storm, the madness of the place shocked even him.

The air was fetid with smoke and sweat and the musky smell of fowl. All the light was concentrated on the ring and gave a devilish leer to the faces. The discordance of contending voices blurred the words until the noise became almost unrecognizable as human speech.

Fifty men crowded about a small arena; two lean cocks sparred in a flurry of spurs and feathers. Man circled the group, straining his eyes in the darkness.

In the foreground on his left as he entered, two dusty jockeys were touching the butts of their whips together and shouting 'Done!' To the right, a fight was in progress, the two men rolling unnoticed among the shifting legs. At the centre of all, two cocks rose in a mess of feathers and blood, their spurs slicing skilfully through the air.

Man worked his way slowly round the ring, trying to fit himself into the mad rhythm of the place. The uproar filled the building as though the storm had been let in. The watchman could feel it inside his chest, could feel the dirt floor vibrating his feet.

He had entrusted his lanthorn to a drowsy beggar-boy near the door, but he still carried his staff. With it, he levered a way through the press of angered, drunken, bellowing men. He watched every gesture, every movement, trying to guess if this man were left-handed or if that leg seemed lame. The faces could not help him much: they were uniformly distorted by the frenzy of the sport.

Man moved through a dizzying maelstrom of voices.

'I lay four guineas to your beaver, Sir, that this bird picks up and wins!'

'Done, Sir!'

The watchman suddenly felt a hand at his pocket and swung his staff down across a skinny wrist. He heard bone crack.

'The outside bird's blooded, by the eyes of God! He's blooded as a bloss!'

'I'll first see the shape of your money, Sirrah!'

'And I'll see you damned in fire first!'

The watchman passed in front of a pig-faced man with a slit nose and a branded palm. Man knew him and looked quickly away towards the jumping birds. He felt a spray of spit against the back of his neck and a cold fear as he tried to lose himself amongst the gamesters.

'He's downed 'im and workin' 'im right!'

Man saw another he knew, and he steered towards him to take refuge in conversation.

He was a young man, no more than fourteen or fifteen, with the frowning eyes and worried mouth of the student. Even here, he carried a volume underneath his arm. Man could see the pages bristling with bookmarks.

'I am that surprised to see you sporting here, Sir.'

The other turned with a jerk, then smiled sheepishly.

'I could say, Sir, that I ran in here to escape the wind. But the truth is that I find these gatherings oftentimes more instructive than my books. There are the seeds here of every comedy and tragedy imaginable.'

Half the room cheered, while the rest moaned.

'Yet here they grow too wild,' Man shouted, 'never tall nor true.'

The young man nodded, but what he answered was swallowed up by the howling of the game.

The watchman craned his neck to survey the room, then leant towards his friend. 'Have you seen one here who goes bad in the left leg?'

'I have only just come myself.' He waved his hand. 'And who could single one out of this crazed mob?'

Man had to agree. The crowd was never still. It would surge in a body towards the warring cocks, then draw back as if to catch its breath for the next onslaught.

'Take care, Mr Scripture,' Man said, moving off, 'that these seeds should not come to find their roots in you.'

By the time the watchman had made a full circuit of the hall, he was certain that the man whom Sarah Wells had so carefully described to him was not there. Plenty were tall; nearly all of them looked vicious. A few of them stood upon a single leg only; one man had none. But no one seemed close enough for Man to risk confronting him in this wild mob.

He had been here but a quarter of an hour, and he already felt exhausted, drained. The fury of the place beat at him worse than any wind. He felt vulnerable, as if he were in a cage with starving beasts.

A sudden outburst shook the pit as two new cocks were brought into play. The room throbbed with violent excitement.

Man looked into the arena and saw the two birds begin to spar. As he moved towards the door, he noticed a new shadow wavering over the sand in the pit – an outline of a hand holding out what looked to be a watch. The watchman smiled to himself and looked up through the smoke and shadows towards the high ceiling.

The man had been basketed, strung up in a wicker basket according to the rules of cocking, for failure to pay his losses. Now he was leaning dangerously out over the edge of the basket, offering security for his good behaviour, his left leg stuck out awkwardly into the air. He was quivering with frustration and anger, as none of the players took any notice of his bribe.

The watchman studied the face, what he could see of it in the darkness, then made his way to the door. The beggar-boy was sleeping, his thin body curled about the fading warmth of the lanthorn. Man slipped a coin into the boy's shirt, lit his candle from his tinder-box, checked his watch. Almost ten. The man in the basket would not be let down until the end of the mains, after midnight at the earliest. For the watchman to beg the crowd to lower him into his custody now would be suicide. Man would have to come back later.

The dark wildness of the storm seemed wonderfully clear to him after the congested brutality of the Cockpit. Man set out almost gladly to his work. Even the hard trek down Long Ditch into the wind made him feel light, blown clean. His thoughts ran solely upon the remembrance of Sarah Wells.

He had passed through Broken Cross and by the Gate House – resisting the temptation to stop in for a rest, preferring the openness of the night air – before he saw the boy. Man was in the middle of the Broad Sanctuary, when he saw a small figure run out of the entrance to Green's Alley and into the periphery of his light. The watchman stopped him with a shout.

'Let yourself catch up with yourself first, boy!'

He was young, six or seven, but wiry. He was panting and trembling with excitement. His eyes shone wide.

'There's a housewife, Sir, dead – killed to pieces she is!'

'Where?'

The boy pointed behind him at the alley.

'In a iron-shop up Green's, on the left. Light on, no shutters, there's another in there with her what sent me out for help!'

Man guessed the boy must have been making for the Gate House. The watchman hesitated for a second, then laid his staff firmly on the boy's shoulder.

'Run you off, then, to the House and carry back the first Constable you can find!'

Man shoved him along and turned to run towards the alley, the light of his lanthorn jiggling nervously before him.

Chapter 3

It did not blow so hard till twelve o'clock at night, but that most families went to bed, though many of them not without some concern . . .

Although the shop was the only one in the street showing life, Man stopped outside for a moment to lift his lanthorn to the rocking, creaking signboard: 'A. Fletcher – Ironmonger', and an amateurish drawing of an archer shooting an over-sized arrow through a series of hanging iron hoops. The door had been braced half open with a keg, and a weak light flickered out on to the loosened, blackened stones of the street.

The watchman stepped into the shop and set his lanthorn down upon the top of a closed cask. The smooth odour of grease and oil hung motionless in the air, even against the fitful gusts of wind through the door. It would be the kind of shop that could never be properly ventilated, but would hold its own distinctive smell in every corner and within the wood of the floor and the walls.

There was a stub of candle guttering at the back of the shop, set upon a deal-board counter. Even with Man's lanthorn, the room was a disturbing mixture of sickly half-light and stubborn shadow. A confusing variety of iron and hardware crowded the floor with no semblance of arrangement: rakes stood bunched with axles, padlocks swung from spits, chains snaked about watering-cans. Man could feel the heaviness of the place in his chest. He seemed rooted to the spot; even the act of picking up his feet would be an exhausting chore.

Behind the counter could be seen the vague outline of a darkened doorway, so low that a grown man would have to stoop down to pass through. To the right of that, steep stairs ran up into darkness.

The room was heavy with silence, though the wind shook and bothered the house. At his feet, Man could hear the tiny chattering of mice.

A shapeless path meandered through the ironware towards the low counter. A pair of feet, ankles, lower legs lay angled open in the middle of the path. They seemed restful, sleeping.

Man stood over the woman's body and moved his eyes up the lean calves, past the outspread knees and narrow hips, and over the level chest to the face and head which seemed bathed in a pool of shadow – or something darker. He bent down to see, then straightened up and looked away, his stomach buckling.

A long sigh from a rear corner of the shop caught his breath in his throat. His grip on his staff tightened.

The man sat upon a covered barrel, leaning against the wall, his hands clasped straining across his breast. He raised his face when Man came up to him, and the flame of the candle was mirrored in his crooked spectacles.

He looked through the watchman and began speaking in an unnaturally quiet voice, as if he were sedately lecturing upon some mundane subject.

'Now the weather has been remarkable, most remarkable, although you must know that I speak in the main of my own area, which is Upminster. Now May last was an exceeding dripping month, more so than any since sixteen ninety-six –

twenty point seven seven pounds in my tunnel. And my thermometer – whose freezing-point, you must remember, is eighty-four – has been very seldom below one hundred all this winter, and especially within this very month of November.

'And as to the wind, you might say that is the most extraordinary phenomenon to date, and you should be quite right in so saying. I myself have gauged them, gauged them all, by means of a rather clever device of my own making. Now the blow of two years past reached a level of nine degrees by my reckoning; that of sixteen ninety-three, ten. But this one tonight! This shall aspire to fifteen, by my guess, at the smallest! Of course, my good friend, Mr Richard Towneley, out at Lancashire, would be in a better position to determine for you the total effects in the open country. And Mr Winstanley – fortunate soul! – could supply us with all manner of particulars concerning the run of the storm against the Eddystone. Would I were there now to second that good man in his works!'

The watchman let the man prattle on, while he studied him with concern. He was a small man, but strong and healthy, with a beaked nose that had difficulty supporting the warped spectacles. Unconsciously, with a nervous bird-like motion, he would dip his head to the right and arch his shoulder to slide the eyeglasses up his nose. But for the circumstances, the man's distracted twitching would have seemed ludicrous.

Man stilled the shoulder with his hand and spoke gently.

'Might I ask your name, Sir?'

The watchman's words seemed to have to travel far.

'What? Oh, what? Yes, I am the Reverend Mr William Derham, yes. Of Upminster, yes, that is correct to the best of my knowledge.'

Man judged him to be in his mid-forties, but in his shaken condition he looked ancient.

'Do you stay here, Sir?'

'Well, as you say, just a few days, just a few days. I really must be getting back to my vicarage – oh, they simply cannot get along without me – and to my Annie, of course, and little William, too. She is my wife, you understand, and he is my son.'

He sighed deeply and looked up innocently at the watchman.

'Today, you see, really is, well, my birthday – that is to say, a commemoration of the day of my own birth.'

Man nodded helpfully. The wind sped by the open door.

'And some of my new fellows from the Society were very gracious enough to toast me at a really very fine tavern and, well, I am afraid we most of us toasted our noses a shade too redly and it was the best I could do to find my way back here against the wind. The shutters were off, the candle was here, I tried the door and to my great surprise it was not locked. And I had been all the time thinking that I must needs call Mistress Fletcher down from her sleep to unbar the door. But, as I say, all lay quite open. So I came directly in and – and, well, I came upon her lying there. I – I am afraid I was quite sick, there behind that stack of spades.'

He made a brief, vague motion with his head and at the same time pushed up his spectacles again.

'And the boy?'

'Eh? The boy, you say?' His face cleared. 'Oh, well, he appeared quite of a sudden at the street door there, frightened me horribly he did, so I sent him straight on for help. I do pray he shall be safe out there all alone. Just a boy, you know.'

Some colour had returned to the man's face by now, and he seemed a bit more calm.

'And are you to be staying long in the town, Reverend?'

'Oh no, not long at all. Perhaps a few days at the most. But

44

the Society people, you know, have been kind enough to express a desire to hear the revision of my "Artificial Clockmaker". And I must really try to interest them in my newest observations of – of the deathwatch.' He twitched his eyeglasses three times in quick succession. 'And there is a friend of mine – the good Mr Defoe – staying at Spitalfields – who has suffered much of late and upon whom I really must call.'

The watchman noticed a long lull in the wind and then a muffled noise overhead.

'Is there now someone else in the house, Sir?'

The Reverend's narrow face assumed the shape of the letter 'O' and then widened in shock.

'May the Lord help us all, it must be Madam Woodman! She will be up there yet, and she cannot know!'

Man ordered him to wait where he was for the coming of the constable and then hurried towards the stairs. He clambered up through a darkness he could feel against his face.

Two doors, light seeping through the cracks in the one on the right. Man hesitated, unsure of himself – not for fear that the murderer might still be hidden somewhere in the house, but out of a polite wish not to surprise a strange lady alone in her room. Finally, thinking that she could be hurt or killed as well, he tapped once lightly with the tip of his staff and opened the door.

The woman sat sprawled fully dressed in a chair. A candle burned on a table beside her; a wooden sewing-box lay fallen at her feet. There was a sagging bed against one wall and a rear window, shuttered.

She seemed to be asleep, or just waking. The watchman could see the shifting gleam of the candle between her eyelids and, bending over her, the strangely languid movements of unseeing eyes. Her breathing was deep and regular.

She was a handsome woman, young, very small and fragile, but with heavy breasts that Man could not help noticing as they rose and fell. Her lips were pouting open, and he could smell the thick musty breath of sleep.

He touched her and called her name. He found that he was sweating slightly in the cold room.

He shook her shoulder gently, then with more force, feeling the sharp bone under his hand.

'Madam Woodman!'

She jerked upright in the chair and grabbed Man's arm.

'Madam Woodman, I am of the parish watch, and I must speak with you now!'

She was fully awake and still holding his arm tightly.

'I fell asleep. I was made so tired by the wind. Is it late? You are – who?'

'Of the watch, Madam.'

She looked suddenly fearful.

'Is he here, then?'

Man did not understand her. He could feel her fingers digging into his arm.

'You have been here all this evening, in this room?'

'Yes, all.'

'And you have heard nothing, nothing before your sleep?'

'Of what, Sir, besides the wind?'

Up here, the storm seemed closer, more restless.

She held her face close to his, and her breathing bothered him. It felt warm and wet, somehow intimate. The watchman loosed his arm and stepped back.

'It is downstairs, Madam, in the shop, some trouble . . .'

She stood up abruptly and moved against him, her clenched hands upon his chest. The top of her head came to just below his shoulder.

'It is my Joan, then. Tell me, Sir, please, what is it?'

Man wished suddenly that he were downstairs in the darkness of the ironmonger's shop or out in the safe emptiness of the streets, that he had left this part of the work to Constable Burton. It was too much for him. He would never be able to find the right words.

'I am afraid that something terrible has happened here tonight. It is – I believe it is Mrs Fletcher, Madam. She is dead.'

The watchman prayed the woman would not faint, but she only laid her head wearily against his greatcoat and whispered something he could not hear.

Imperceptibly, almost without Man's realizing it, the woman eased her body into his until he could feel the breathing of her stomach against his groin. She leaned on him as if she were losing the strength to stand. His right hand still held the staff; with his left, he lowered her back into the chair and felt his palm brush across the side of her breast.

'Madam, we must vacate the house. Do you hear? Are there other stairs to the street? You should not see . . .'

She waved a hand distractedly towards the side of the house that had the staircase Man had just climbed.

'A door at the end of the hall. There are steps outside.'

For no reason, Man crouched down at the woman's feet, laid his staff on the floor, and began to gather bunches of fabric into the sewing-box. He ran his hand across the splintered wood in search of needles. It seemed absurdly important to him that everything be replaced.

'I must go down to meet the Constable. It is better that you stay here. I will come back for you.'

He put the sewing-box in her lap.

As he was leaving the room, the woman murmured, 'Help me,' but he did not turn round.

Downstairs in the ironmonger's shop, the Reverend William Derham had not moved. Now, he appeared to be praying.

The boy whom Man had sent on to the Gate House was perched on top of a bulging sack near the body. He was chewing something and staring down at the head of the dead woman with the bored patience of a cow.

Constable Charles Burton was standing next to a leaning stack of spades, examining the floor by the light of Man's lanthorn. He turned a grim face towards the watchman.

'Ah, 'tis George Man, then. As I thought when the lad comes to me at the Gate House. What other night-walker would be so buck-mad as to be out naked this blustering night?'

His soiled wig already lay askew, but he gave it another half-turn beneath his hat, bringing a curl over his left eye. He stood at the head of the body and waited for Man to join him, then waved the lanthorn over the woman.

'But 'tis bad enough work thou hast uncovered for us tonight, George.'

They spoke together over the body between them, sometimes glancing down at the chest or the limbs. By silent consent, neither man would look at the face, nor would they talk directly of the injuries. Neither had the stomach of the boy, who might have been waiting for fish to rise and bite.

Constable Burton gestured with his big head at the spades, and his wig spun back into place on his smoothly shaved skull.

'And there's the tool what did it, put back right as ninepence.' Man saw that the blade of one of the standing spades was spread with dark gore. 'Thou couldst not have chosen in a month a better to make a mess of a fine neb.'

The watchman tried again to make himself look at the face, but could not.

The Constable pointed at the floor beneath the body.

'Got her round about closing-up time, I should say.'

Man felt ashamed of himself. He must have seen before that the dead woman lay sprawled across a pair of old rain-eaten shutters, but it had meant nothing to him then.

'Have you talked with the Reverend yet?' Man said in a low voice, motioning towards the rear of the shop.

'Aye, but not much to be got by him, I'm certain. Poor man's quite taken through the centre by this – as any of us might have been, come tripping upon such a sight in this dark house.'

The Constable scowled round at the shadows that seemed to be built above the level of the iron. At night, the ironmonger's shop held two sets of merchandise, one real and one of shadow. The watchman knew Constable Burton was as fearless a man as any, in almost any situation; but he knew, too, that he felt a particularly sensitive dread of spirits.

'The vicar's, as I understand it, lodging here these times. Dost thou know of any others, George?'

Man had all but forgotten the woman upstairs.

'One, I think. There is a woman above – a widow, Madam Woodman. I roused her from her first sleep. She claims to have been in the evening and to have heard nothing save the wind.'

'Pretty?'

Man pretended not to have noticed the eagerness in the Constable's voice. Charles Burton was close to fifty years old, a successful fellmonger with a faithful wife and grown children; but Man had found him more than once, standing in the shade of a low, loud bagnio with some slight figure whose head was lowered into the darkness. The watchman had never thought him a vicious man, but he knew his interests.

'Is this a widow, too, do we know?' Man dipped his head at the body. 'Or is there a husband still?'

'Aye, he's one that's opposite to you two gents: he takes his breeches off *before* he comes into his house!'

Both Man and the Constable stared at the boy in surprise, but he only shrugged in wonder at their ignorance.

Constable Burton eyed the six-year-old with distrust.

'And shouldst thou not, my fine mannikin, have been long since at thy home and pulling at thy mamma's titty?'

The boy tried to think of an apt reply, then settled upon sticking out his tongue.

A long and echoing crack overhead caught their attention. The wind seemed to have shifted or the house itself shifted within the battering persistence of the storm. A high shuffling could be heard from the roof, and the street seemed crowded with tumbling wreckage.

The Constable waded through the piled iron and came back with a coarse, grease-spotted tarpaulin. He made a move towards the body, then forced the canvas on the watchman.

'Shalt be thy work, George, to cover this sad dame against the eyes of the widow, when I shall carry her down here . . .'

'There is an outside stair—' interrupted Man.

'In this blow? Bethink thyself betimes. We must have these souls off to the Gate House before the bones of this house rumble about their ears. And we shall need God's grace to land ourselves whole behind stone as it is.' He paused and looked sympathetically at the watchman. 'And I must ask thee, George Man, to hold this place still on thy own for the husband's return. What's the clock?'

Man checked his watch: almost eleven and the half.

'If he hath not come within the hour, shut up the house as best may be against the coroner's sitting on the morrow and bring thyself to the Gate House.' He glanced at the woman's body. 'This wants a minute's talking betwixt us.'

The Constable hurried up the stairs.

For a moment, Man stood absolutely still. He was suddenly conscious of the chorus of sounds about him: the heavy running of the Constable, the irregular moaning of the Reverend, the boy's soft chewing, and over all the ceaseless rattling of the storm. Then he bent down and began to arrange the tarpaulin over the corpse.

'What's that, then?'

The watchman followed the boy's pointing finger. He frowned, trying to see, then brought the lanthorn down from the top of the cask where Constable Burton had set it.

Across the front of the dress, between the small bumps of the breasts, lay a shapeless stain. A thin rivulet extended downward to the belly. Man reached out a trembling hand: it was dry, but slightly sticky and granular to the touch. The light of the lanthorn gleamed wetly upon what was left of the woman's face, and Man tasted a hot bitterness at the back of his throat.

'From the mouth, perhaps,' he said weakly, unfolding the canvas over the body, 'or from the brain.'

He stood up quickly and felt the floor of the shop heave under his feet. He fumbled for his pipe and lit it from the lanthorn, scorching his face.

He was sucking hungrily at the smoke, when a high-pitched, whining voice spoke to him from the open front door.

'I am afraid, Sir, that my wife does not at any time allow smoking within the house.'

None of the citizens of Westminster could remember a time when the Gate House Prison had not stood across the street at the end of the houses at the entrance to the Abbey, one archway leading into Tothill Street and another, to the left, lying opposite the entrance into Dean's Yard. It had been used as their prison for centuries, and some said that the man who had once stood before the Gate House Prison – or in it – could never go anywhere without carrying a part of Westminster with him.

Tonight, George Man was especially glad of its thick walls and stout timbers. He was sitting now in a cramped guard-room, savouring a postponed pipe and a large cup of burning rum provided by the Constable. Man was near the fire. The boy and the Reverend were snoring in unison from the depths of a blanket on the floor. On a stool in the farthest corner of the room – as if he could find comfort only in the cold and the dark – sat the ironmonger.

The scene in the shop in Green's Alley had been absurd.

'I will ask you, Sir, to step out of my shop at once, if you do not think to trade here.'

Alan Fletcher had advanced upon the watchman with a face blackening in anger, coming to a stop with his wife's outstretched legs lying unseen between them.

Man had studied him in the sickly light of the ironmonger's shop. Alan Fletcher was a short and flabby man who seemed to have kept much of his baby fat, although the watchman guessed him to be already in his early or middle thirties. He looked weak and defenceless, the kind of man whom others would bump against in doorways without even thinking to ask his pardon.

It was his skin that had bothered Man the most. It was too white, pasty and colourless, as porous as a sponge. It gave the eerie impression that a finger poked anywhere into the puffy flesh would leave a permanent indentation. The skin sagged on the face, and the body seemed to have been ladled into the threadbare clothes like warm dough.

The ironmonger had faced Man, shivering with wrath, but not daring to meet his eyes.

'I demand a reason, Sir, for your stopping here at this hour. I am the man of this house, and I will know it. I will!'

The watchman had almost given way to nervous giggling, as Alan Fletcher had stood puffing himself up like an exasperated cock in the ring.

Man had made no answer, only nodded once towards the floor and then looked quickly up to catch the ironmonger's reaction.

And the husband's reaction had puzzled him at the time, and it puzzled him still.

It had seemed genuine enough: the spasm of shock, the wordless grief, the sob. Fletcher had turned away and refused to look at the body. It must be his wife, he had murmured, because only death could have forced her to leave the shop open and unguarded.

Then he had stood motionless in a corner, until the Constable had finally come downstairs with the other woman.

Judith Woodman had avoided looking at anybody, stationing herself as close to the open front door as she could without actually stepping out.

Constable Burton, whose bear's body seemed unbalanced without the Constable's painted staff of authority, had run through a series of preliminary questions in a voice hurried by fear and excitement. And the ironmonger had responded in a clockwork monotone.

'I was out, yes, as I am every evening. First looking after whatever iron might have been blown free by the wind, although I had no fortune there this night. Then, as is my wont, I took company with some of my fellows who travel the taverns and the coffee-houses together. Less than an hour, though,' he had added quickly, 'much less: there is no going abroad in this blow.'

Had he in that time passed by his shop at all?

'Oh no, no. I kept myself nearer to the river.'

Had any particular gentlemen been expected to call?

The ironmonger had looked momentarily confused.

'No, I think not. Who could have wanted to come? My few friends know my hours, and my – my wife looked for no one. Unless, of course, Madam Woodman was waiting for someone. She was here, I think.' And Fletcher had turned and raised a hand weakly in the direction of the woman standing alone and silent at the door.

Any cash or notes wanting?

The ironmonger had then stepped through the low door behind the counter and brought back a dented tin box, broken open. He had said nothing more, but Man had seen him staring at the rounded back of the widow.

Now, in the snug warmth of the guard-room, Man had just begun thinking of questioning the ironmonger further – if he were still awake – when Constable Burton suddenly came in from outside, bringing a roomful of freezing air in with him.

In the Constable's walk was a smug excitement and relaxation that, for no reason he could name, made the watchman want to get up without a word and go out to his work.

'As tasty a dish of pudding as I've stirred up this season, my boy!' he whispered huskily into Man's face, then hooked a chair closer to the fire with his foot and dropped himself into it with a satisfied grunt. 'Thou wast the finest fool to let the moment fly thee by like that. But no matter: there's likely more than enough lickings yet to be had from that sweet pot!'

The Constable stretched out his legs towards the fire and rubbed himself luxuriously. He glanced over his shoulder at the ironmonger sitting alone in the dark and lowered his voice.

'Thou and I, George, ought to have us a word ready for our good coroner, when he sits tomorrow, on this sad affair.'

'*If* he sits tomorrow, Sir, if Westminster still stands.'

'Ha! Never fear for that, my boy. Our dry-fisted Mr Fry's

awake in his duties, though a man that hath more hair than wit about him. And he'll be wanting some story from us concerning what we found in Green's Alley tonight. As it stands now, I have not the first word for him. Nor for these folk from the shop: I hold them here tonight to save them from this killing wind; but what to do with them when the storm dies out?'

The puzzled expression on the Constable's face was new to Man.

'The boy, surely, can be got safely home?'

'Oh, Isaac, yes: he's a ranging but a goodly lad. I can send him on; I know his father. Though I doubt not but Mr Hervey's too deep in drink and in lifting his leg to waste much thought on his only.'

Man offered Constable Burton his pouch, and the two of them stoked their pipes. In the background, the wind could be heard swelling in its strength and depth. It reminded the watchman of the one time in his life when he had stood listening to the sea at night and feeling totally unnerved and helpless.

'What is your thought, then, Sir, on the death of this poor woman?'

The Constable rubbed himself once more, this time with more urgency. He was getting restless again.

'We know the time, as the man hath said his wife shut up at nine each night. We know that he himself was out at business with two or three of his mates. The Reverend, of course, will be spoke for by his fellows from the Society.'

'So the widow alone was at the house with Mrs Fletcher.'

Burton gave a soft chuckle and wrinkled his face at the watchman.

'Thou must learn, George Man, before thou art at thy majority, that a well-wetted dame such as Madam Woodman will tell one thing to a boy and two-halves of another to a man.

Under my stroking hand, she admits to having flown out and down the side-stairs tonight and being abroad from some time before nine to some before ten. Then she slept for thy coming.'

'And where did she go?'

'Where else, then, but to the stiff and stout? She's been at the widow-lay three year.'

'And she saw nothing off in the shop's being lit and open at her coming in?'

The Constable stared cross-eyed for a moment at the burning end of his pipe, then shrugged his shoulders without interest.

'Who sees his own house, especially with his eyes full of wind?'

Man thought he saw a crease of doubt remaining in the Constable's broad, carefree face, but he could not be sure. And the watchman felt his own uncertainty about why Madam Woodman had lied to him.

'And did you, Sir,' Man asked after a pause, 'come close enough to the lady to learn the name of the man she met?'

Feeling somehow confused, the watchman wondered if there had been a sarcastic note in his question and if he had really intended one. The Constable had noticed nothing.

'Women of that kidney, George, are like the hand-shy cow that'll skit, if she be not milked well.' Constable Burton grinned widely. 'Now, no dame shall will to give out wide report among her men; but, beneath the proper dildoing—' he dropped his voice still lower and leaned forward – 'well, I shall tell thee, George, and thee alone, that Madam Woodman stepped out this night for a gay moment with one Zachary Trippuck, a sometime sack-weaver from Woolstaple Market way. I myself have heard some of that man – and nothing clean.'

Over the Constable's shoulder, Man could see the dark, still figure of Alan Fletcher. The ironmonger sat stooped over, staring blankly before him. He seemed far enough away, both in distance and in mood, not to be able to hear, but Man brought his head close to the Constable's.

'And this man shall speak for the widow?'

'Like as not.' The Constable spoke casually, but for the first time he looked worried. 'Yet Mr Trippuck's word is as water to most good men in this city.'

The watchman looked at Constable Burton and suddenly felt a twinge of repugnance towards his usually jovial superior. When Man spoke, there was an edge in his voice.

'I do not wish, Sir, to darken the name of Madam Woodman nor to set myself against your own favouritism. But we have a woman killed here, and that as wretchedly as any I have seen. We must both agree, I think, that the Reverend is a wholly hurtless man. Mr Fletcher, by his own word and by those of his friends, was away at the time, as he swears to be most nights. And the streets are mostly untenanted tonight, because of the storm. That leaves the widow at least the closest to the ironmonger's shop at the hour for closing-up.' Now Man could not keep his hurt pride from squeaking childishly in his voice. 'There is no guarantee, Sir, that the woman who deceived a boy tonight may not also have deceived a man. There is not always the best of truth to be found in some women and that but rarely in their lifted-heels promises, Sir!'

Man hurried to knock out his pipe and refill it, all the while looking stubbornly into the fire.

Constable Burton's face had grown very red during Man's speech, and his teeth had ground down hard upon the stem of his pipe. He held his breath for a moment, then let it out in a rushing sigh, wagging his great head tolerantly at the watchman.

'I have known thee, George Man, almost as long as thou

hast been at the watch; and I know thee for a serious, well-headed young man. Thou hast more of sense in thy breeches than any other hour-grunter in Westminster. But I have some few years behind my belt, thou must give me that; and I do know more of men and women than only prick and princock. Now we both of us saw the ironmonger's wife, and a redder sight I hope never to see in my last days. Now I ask thee: was that a woman's work, the work of one whose head comes barely to my belly? Or more: dost thou think that such work could belong to the hand of a dame such as Judith Woodman, a lady who is as meek and soft and serviceable as my own youngest girl? No, Sir; thou'd have me as soon believe 'twas the day-work of the good Reverend or –' he whispered and arched his eyebrows to indicate the man at his back – 'of the hornless husband himself. And I shall believe that, Sir, when our new Queen herself strides through the dark streets at the head of the hardest press-gang in town!

'What hath been unminded, George, in this thy age as it was not in mine own, is that amongst the most of the people lies an easy division between those who strike and those who yield, the man that takes the wall from thee with a curse and the man that surrenders it to thee with a smile. The choleric will fell thee at once or haunt thee for thy life with his hatred. The sanguinary will forgive thee thy injuries and love thee for thy faults. And the man who, like our ironmonger, feels himself filled with watery phlegm, shall not be strong enough even to meet thee in thy face. And the like with the women, George. How a man is born is how he dies. There can be no change at bottom. I'll not believe it, Sir, I'll not! Madam Woodman could not abuse her friend and landlady so, nor even be a party to it. Sooner the poxed devil himself kiss my blind cheeks!'

The Constable sat back and wiped the sweat from his jowls.

Outside, the wind howled through the Gate House; inside, the boy snuffled in his sleep.

Man could see the ironmonger nodding on his stool.

'Then who, Sir?'

'Why, then, why not some quick Tumbler or rough shop-pad, running maddened before this hell-born storm? Mind thee, George, that in Green's Alley the Fletcher man made search in that back room for the shop's money box and found it cleaned. A woman alone in a lighted shop, some loose crew passes by in the emptied street, a surprise, a struggle, and she finds her death. 'Tis a nightly scene, as thou well knowest, and no night better than this. If Coroner Fry should wish to fix the hand in this red work, he must look into any of our Stop-Hole Abbeys, and not into the houses of our quiet folk.'

The Constable fell silent, ruminating upon his smoked-out pipe.

Man rose wearily to his feet.

'Art thou thinking still of watching the streets alone in the body of this storm?'

'I am, Sir. There may be need.'

'More fool thou, then. But keep thy eye open for any near the Green's Alley and for this Trippuck bully who is said to rule the streets after midnight. And get thee back to the ironmonger's in the morning for the coroner's word!'

Man nodded thoughtfully, took up his staff, lit his cold lanthorn.

At the door, he heard the Constable's voice again, now growing sleepy.

'And mind the poor farthing-anglers on your way past the Prison walls.'

Man said he would.

As he passed beneath the high dark slots in the wall, he saw a single cap swinging and twisting at the end of a long string. In the louder screaming of the wind, the felon's plea came down to him as an angry demand: 'Pray remember the goddamned prisoners, for the love of Christ!'

Man tucked a penny into a fold of the cap, pulled the string, and turned his back to the rising storm.

Chapter 4

But about one, or, at least, by two o'clock, 'tis supposed few people, that were capable of any sense of danger, were so hardy as to lie in bed . . . And yet, in this general apprehension, nobody durst quit their tottering habitations; for, whatever the danger was within doors, it was worse without.

The citizens of Westminster could not sleep. They walked their floors fully dressed, stopping every few moments to listen with straining ears. It was the chimneys that frightened them most. They feared lying in bed, deep asleep, and then waking at the last instant to see a sudden shower of bricks come crashing through the splintering ceiling directly at their faces. Some had already dreamt it: they had started up to find shattered stones mixed with dust and paint descending slowly like a pall over their eyes, the awful massive weight flattening the chest and crushing the breath, the fall bearing them downward through bed and floor into the downstairs room and into a circle of shocked faces, and still further down into the quiet stone foundation itself. Then they had woken a second time to a darkened room and a moaning house, their bodies clammy with sweat, the limbs twitching helplessly, to lie awake uncertain which was the nightmare and which was the night.

Next they feared fire. The wind would nurse it and lengthen it from room to room and from house to house. Some of the people sat up in the dark with no fire; others set their candles in iron pails and shouted angrily every time someone with a flaring dress or a hanging wig passed by too near. The leather buckets had been filled early in the evening, drenched sheets left hanging near the door. At least one window in every house had been unfastened for escape. Everyone wore shoes.

But even the dread of a collapsing house was preferred to the moving horror of the streets. They peered through their shutters into the darkness and knew there was nowhere to run. The streets seemed to have narrowed with sunset, the buildings had grown fatally high. Suddenly, they could not remember which of the side-alleys were blind and which were open. They tried to calculate distances in the dark: fifty yards to that cellar-opening, a hundred to the corner. They measured their stride on the floor of the hall; some exercised their legs. They showed a quick light out the window and tried to estimate the trajectories of vaulting tiles and sign-boards, scraps of iron and twisting sheets of lead: two hundred yards, at the least.

The old were set in the securest corners beneath fortifications of the thickest blankets. Children were herded under low tables, where they curled up and went casually to sleep and were forgotten in the panic.

In some houses, women laboured to give birth, hurried on by the hurrying wind. Their husbands knelt over them and felt sick, their hands stiff and slippery. The midwives all stayed home.

In others, those who lay dying wondered bitterly why they could not be allowed to pass in peace.

At the river, merchants sat huddled with watermen and totalled their losses. Mooring chains stretched across the river strained, snapped. At the Nore, two men-of-war and twelve sail of the Queen's hired ships foundered crazily before the gale. Seven hundred sail cast loose and driven together between Shadwell and Limehouse. Five hundred wherries bobbed and tossed. And near Blackfriars, Henry Dow, having clattered down drunk into the cabin of a barge, slept thoughtlessly on as he was rocked and steered towards the Bridge.

Among the streets of Westminster, the wind spread trouble randomly from place to place.

In a corner-house at Broken Cross, the gable ends projecting over the street shattered and fell upon the greengrocer who was about to run into the shelter of the doorway. He was stunned; the watchman revived him with water carried in his hat from the communal water-tap in the street.

A distiller in Long Ditch, with his wife and maidservant, were buried in the rubbish of a fallen roof. Man and wife were rescued, but the young watchman could not save the maid.

In Duffin's Alley, a plasterer refused to leave his shaking house and had to be removed by force – the watchman bearing him across his shoulders like a sack of meal – minutes before the walls caved in.

Two women at Bell Yard were injured – the first by running out of the house into the street, where she was struck senseless by a gliding signboard; the second by staying inside, where she was cut by blowing glass. Both received aid from the watchman, who himself seemed even more battered and exhausted than they.

And in King Street, opposite the end of Gardiner's Lane, a fire broke out in the hallway of a small house. The widow and her three daughters stood crying half-naked in the street. After the watchman had smothered the flames with his greatcoat, the ladies invited him in for a dish of geneva, but he said he had to move on. They watched him disappear down King Street, and the girls talked excitedly about his strong hands and his fine head and his courage.

'Then eat it up while it's still hot, sweetheart, and I'll fetch you another bowlful. There's nothing finer to hold inside of you on a night as dark as this one.'

Man nodded and bent to the steaming tripe-soup. He was bone-tired, but he could feel the thick, rank-smelling soup settling into his stomach and spreading its heat throughout his body. And the cups of cock ale which he took between spoonfuls sent a pleasing lightness to his head that helped him forget his tiredness.

He had turned into Antelope Alley at two o'clock in order to replenish his supply of candles from the stock in his room. The air in the closed street had seemed somewhat stiller. He needed a rest. When he had noticed a faint light burning behind the shutters of the tripe-shop, he had been taken by a sudden craving for the tripe whose cooking filled his upstairs room all day. Even tonight, the wind could do little against the indestructible smell: it met him at least five paces from the closed door.

Man was sitting now in an enclosed space behind the main room of the shop. The dimensions of the walls were only slightly greater than those of the table. The trapped air was stale with a smell of organs and blood that never changed, except to grow again as pungent in midsummer. Even the table, clean as it was always kept, seemed sweaty to the touch, as if the tripe had been in the soil from which the wood had grown. Although it had never bothered him, Man knew that some of the other people in the alley considered the tripe-sellers to be as malodorous as their wares; he had seen some talking with the woman out in the open air, their heads turned carefully to one side. Yet the tripe-sellers themselves never cared, as long as they continued to do good trade.

Dorothy Puncheon ladled out another bowl of soup for Man, filling it until the rich broth slopped over on to the table. She was a fat and healthy woman, always cheerful, unashamedly salacious, with fleshy neck and arms that could not easily be distinguished from the gut hanging from the walls. She was neither young nor old; she watched over Man like a mother and teased him like a lover.

Her husband, Nicholas, was the quiet one. He suffered from a natural lethargy which seemed to make even speaking an impossible chore. Though thin, the flesh on his face drooped flabbily into an unchangeable mask of mourning. His outlook upon the whole of life was so consistently dismal that nobody could see it as anything but comical.

It was the husband who had kept the house lighted and himself and his wife awake. He had had a feeling, he said: a premonition. The house would fall tonight, in whole or in part, of that he had no doubt. But before it did, the knives would begin gently swaying at the hooks, and that was to be their signal to run. And if they lay upstairs wrapped in their sleep, or even if they were awake, how – he would be most pleased to know – how were they to know when the last moment came? The fall would catch them unawares and lay them lower than sodden tripe.

Nicholas Puncheon was sitting at the table with Man, while the woman fussed back and forth in a tattered nightdress and her husband's nightcap. He sat dressed in his best street-clothes, his cheeks sagging more pathetically than ever, one foot tapping rhythmically underneath the table. His fear had made him restless, even talkative.

'Know the man.'

The watchman had just told the tripe-sellers of the night's events in Green's Alley.

Man looked up from the last few drops of his soup.

'Who do you mean, Sir? The ironmonger, Alan Fletcher?'

'The same.'

Man had lived for nearly a year now over the tripe-shop, and he knew of the immense difficulties in trying to hold a connected conversation with Nicholas Puncheon. Tonight, although the storm made him talk, it also made him unusually restive and distracted. The watchman had never seen the tripe-man in such a state.

'Might I ask how you come to know him, Sir?'

'A friend who trades in iron. Or, rather, tries to. And when that fails him – and that's most often – he deals in that which rightly belongs elsewhere.'

'With the man, Fletcher, do you mean?'

Nicholas Puncheon cocked his head alertly.

'Did you hear that? The sound of bricks unsettling above, was it not?' His feet tapped furiously, and he raised the candle to study the ceiling. 'Cheapest wood from God's green forest, that. What?'

'Had your friend such dealings with Alan Fletcher?' Man coaxed him.

'With him amongst others. In some streets, Fletcher's known for it. Watches and goldsmith's notes, mainly.'

'The wife, too, then?'

Dorothy Puncheon had been standing at the door to the shop, wiping her hands on her nightdress. Now she broke in scornfully.

'More she than he, if I know her. Not to speak ill, but I've heard of her as cold as any of their iron and twice as hard. She'd of sold the child, if it'd been unlucky enough to come to light.'

Her husband seemed to consider this, slowly and ponderously. Man could see the flesh of his face composing itself to speak.

'No, Madam, I'd say she's all you say, and more; but I can't think to have heard any blacken her own honesty, rough as it is. She wants it all, that's true enough, but she's said to want it straight.'

It unnerved Man to hear Joan Fletcher spoken of as if she were still living. He had seen her.

'No,' the tripe-man continued, rolling his eyes at each chance creak of the house, 'I'll warrant you it was the man himself that ran it, and that on his wife's blind side.'

Man recalled the ironmonger's shop and its dark poverty.

'He does not seem to have much prospered from it.'

'Yes, I've heard somewheres that that trade has fallen down on him of late. Not the city's fault, mind: with the war at us, there's notes about for any stray hand. No, as like as not the Mistress one day spied a thread on it and pulled. She would not live with it, that woman.'

A hollow thump resounded through the house and brought Nicholas Puncheon half way to his feet. He froze in a runner's crouch and stared at the knives that hung motionless against the wall. His wife clucked her tongue and pushed him firmly back on to his chair. The foot-tapping started up again.

'He followed her, then, did he?' the watchman asked Dorothy Puncheon.

'Aye, the market-women love to talk on that. They can name you every man in Westminster that don't have it in their backs to stand upright in their homes. And the ironmonger in Green's Alley's as bad-spoke as any of them. He takes in the shop's coin and hands it straight to the petticoat.'

'And his private earnings from the notes?'

'Oh no, that'd be kept stuck deep in his own breeches, where he used to keep the nutmegs.' She gave a deep-bellied laugh at the watchman's blush, but then became serious. 'Not but there's more that the ladies bandy about that one. He's said to have a keen edge hidden in him, an anger that sparks out of him at a wink. A peevish, petty sort of soul that'll let almost anything set his back up. But there's always more smoke than fire to that sort: all "great cry and little wool", as the Ruffin himself shouted when he sheared the hogs!'

Man looked up at the broad, good-humoured face of the tripe-woman and enjoyed her infectious healthfulness. Sitting here with the Puncheons served to offset the effects of everything he had seen and felt in Green's Alley and at the Gate House Prison.

As though he were talking mostly to himself, the husband said: 'And those are the men that wear one face in the shop during the day and another at night in the streets.'

The watchman may not have heard. He was thinking of the lodger, Judith Woodman, and wondering why – if he had felt so uncomfortable at his meeting with her – he wanted very much to see her again.

'There is a lodger, one Judith Woodman, who may be in some way involved.'

Man had spoken hesitatingly to Dorothy Puncheon, but it was her husband who responded first.

'Knew her man, as coarse a fellow as I'd ever wish to meet. That was, oh, four, five years ago. He dealt some in iron, too, with A. Fletcher. Most likely in some other ware, too, but I don't know of it. He was well-basted for his troubles – round about the century, it was – and died of it a few days after. Little good his own oaken towel did him at that juncture.'

'Was he receiving as well?'

'Who's to say? I seem to recall that he had some relation to the stew-trade, but that was kept close-silented.'

'From his wife?'

Dorothy Puncheon answered, and her voice sounded uncommonly harsh.

'Can't be done with that one! She's the lady to know before any which side of her bread is buttered, and like enough 'tis the slice she's taken from your own mouth, too. Whatever business her man may've been at would've been known to her even before him. And such a small and helpless little minx that she is! Ties herself up to the nearest rod like a filly to a post. I see her time and again in the King Street and give her a wide walk-by. There's no secret to it: Judith Woodman may look as if the butter wouldn't melt in her mouth, but it's well-known that the cheese'll never choke her.' Dorothy Puncheon looked critically at the watchman's discomfort. 'Aye, poor lad, so she's worked herself on you as well, then, has she? Remember what I say, George Man, and keep yourself far off that dame. She makes no distinction, not even between the position of the beard. Do you know that one milk-woman tells me that the bony one spends more of her nights in the widow's bed, lying head to toe, than she does in her man's.'

Man noticed the taste of rising gorge in his mouth.

'The ironmonger's wife?'

'Aye, that's my meaning,' she said, nodding and opening her red eyes wide. 'If you're meaning to look for who did the Fletcher woman, don't forget about our widow. A woman can feel the bed-love for another woman as easy as for a man. And the hate. Else why has Judith Woodman stayed on so long at Green's Alley? She's young enough; she's time enough for a second man or even a third, but there she sits. Too much of a sister in the house, to my mind.'

'How long has she been lodging there, then?'

'Why, the three years since her own man went down. And

she went straight to Green's Alley, never looking right or left, much as she'd been called to it. There were rooms less dear elsewhere, as there have been since; but I wager she found what she wanted there.'

'Had they known each other previous?'

'The women? No, I think not, not but through their men. But they had that in common between the two of them: a small enough liking for their own husbands. Woodman was said to be the only man his wife would never lay for, as she was about the only dolly in Westminster he'd not enjoyed. A fine family, the four of them.'

Man turned his cup round in a wet circle on the table.

'The widow is a handsome woman. Two of them in the one house . . . I wonder that Mrs Fletcher never felt a worry for her husband.'

'What? For that mollying pup?' Dorothy Puncheon gave a genuinely uproarious howl and started to clear the table. As she moved off towards the kitchen, she could still be heard snickering to herself.

Man stood up to go. Nicholas Puncheon, for all his fear of the storm, seemed about to give in at last to the heavy lethargy that so often perturbed his customers. The watchman had to speak his name twice to rouse him.

'Do you know, Mr Puncheon, if any were ever charged with the dying of the man, Woodman? I myself cannot recall the circumstances.'

The tripe-man dreamily fingered the loose skin of his cheeks. His eyes were glazed with sleep and worry.

'No, none that I can call to mind. Likely the dust of the street was the only witness. Know where it happened, though; down in Channel Row, where Woodman spent the half or more of his times. Seraglios dark enough for his taste in that neighbourhood. And he was set upon in the very face of one of them by three or four with sticks. Mrs Woodman couldn't name him when he was carried home, so bloodied-up he was. Heard that he could still talk, but wouldn't. Some said he'd no need to, that his woman knew enough for the both of them. But she never talked neither, though that don't hold much with her. She does all her saying through her hairy kettle.'

The tripe-man laughed – a dry, broken cackle that went no deeper than his throat. It was the first laugh Man had heard from him since a pillorying outside the Royal Exchange in July.

'Did he leave the woman well-settled?'

'Nary the ghost of a guinea, Sir. Yet she's never gone begging, though the small sewing she follows can't keep her. But she's one who'll never go without, as long as there's a buck nearby to pay her.'

The watchman left him staring morosely at the still unmoving knives and tapping his foot spasmodically. Dorothy Puncheon let Man out into the windy street, slipping something into the pocket of his greatcoat before she closed the door. Outside, Man stood and smiled down at the fresh trotter wrapped in wetted paper. He would breakfast well.

He moved off towards the open end of Antelope Alley, the warm pig's foot a comfortable heaviness in his pocket. But he was thinking of the widow, Judith Woodman.

If Nicholas Puncheon had not made mention of it, Man would never have thought to bother walking up the length of Channel Row. It lay, in fact, outside his area, and it had a reputation for uncontrolled drunkenness and sudden violence. But a freak twist of wind had carried him out of Antelope Alley, across King Street, and into the entrance to the Market, and he had made for Channel Row thinking more of shelter than of work. And it was there that he found the woman.

It was at a place near the bottom of the street, where the road was rough and slanted towards the river. There, between two dark houses, was a walking space that should not have been there, that could serve no good purpose. Mounds of rubbish overflowed from its mouth, and the wind plucked at them.

As Man stepped past, hugging the wall for windbreak, he heard a hidden moaning that could have been a dog or the wind or someone in pain.

He found her in an accidental niche in the side-wall, curled up with her head lowered to her chest and her hands clasped between her thighs. She must have crawled or rolled there without thinking, like a hurt animal that wants to retreat to some place where it can feel something solid against its back. She was only half-conscious; and, when Man deflected the light of his lanthorn upon her face, she shrank back whimpering and fainted away again. Her eyelids fluttered, and her breathing sounded sick.

There were the marks of hands upon her face, the lips were cracked and bruised, and the line of the jaw was crooked. A quick examination told the watchman that her back and limbs were unbroken. Her clothes had been ripped in places, but not torn off. She had no stockings or shoes, and the bottoms of her feet were cut and bleeding.

Man crouched down beside the woman, wondering what had brought her out alone into the storm. He had already guessed what had happened to her. It was nothing new for the watchman to find women – young and old, some mere girls – lying abused and beaten in the street. The night-streets were savage enough for men; for women, they were unendurable. He had picked up dozens of them, raped and bleeding, and revived them with salt of hartshorn. But they were the luckiest: some of them he could not wake.

72

Working quickly, the watchman ran his staff through the belt at his back, hooked his burning lanthorn to his side, and bent to lift her in his arms. She was not a big woman, but her body sagged limply at the hips and her skirts wrinkled to her waist, baring her thighs. She was naked underneath. And in the close air between the houses, Man caught the bitter smell of badly singed hair.

Feeling foolish and ashamed, but not wanting to set her back down upon the wet earth, the watchman dipped his head and settled her clothes over her legs with his teeth.

Coming out into the open street with the woman already growing heavier in his arms, Man realized he could make none of the watch-houses in this wind. The houses here looked dark and forbidding. He could dimly remember an apothecary's shop somewhere along the right-hand side of Channel Row, so he headed northward up the street, the wind trying to tug the woman from his arms.

The house was a small, neat one that belonged in a better part of Westminster. Man made out an oddly shaped signboard and the name, 'Charles Dickinson'. He recognized the name with some surprise. His frantic kicking against the bottom of the door finally brought a light glimmering through the seams of the shutters and a tired voice through a grilled hole in the woodwork. The watchman put his mouth to the hole and begged for help.

He was led immediately into an extremely tidy shoproom, the walls lined with dark glass jars, earthenware pots, and open wooden boxes. The air was thick and clinging with the aroma of fresh plants and dried herbs. A large pair of scales gleamed dully on the polished counter.

The apothecary wasted no time. Silently, he directed Man to carry the woman to a cot in a narrow room at the back of the shop, then pushed him gently back into the front room. The woman moaned feebly, but did not wake up.

The watchman unhooked his lanthorn and set it down upon the counter, laid his staff aside. He stood then savouring the rich smells of the air. Ever since his boyhood, Man had always loved the atmosphere of the apothecary's shop with its orderly collection of unknown medicines and its grotesquely shaped bottles and flasks. But he had also retained enough of a childish fear of illness to make him wish the apothecary would hurry and let him return to the open streets.

In a few minutes, the man stepped out and without a word began selecting ingredients from the hundreds crowding the shelves. He had left his candle behind and Man's lanthorn gave off only a half-light, but the apothecary moved quickly and confidently about the room, gathering his materials by means of touch and memory.

The watchman was left alone again. He walked uneasily over to a clock that was softly ticking beside a beaker filled with greenish, spongy roots. It was a quarter to four.

The apothecary came out and motioned Man to be quiet and to follow him up the set of stairs at the back corner of the shop. They came to a cramped and airless room on the first floor that Man supposed was the apothecary's study. In one corner, grey with dust, sat a complicated machine of toothed wheels and springs and crisscrossing levers that was used for correcting rounded shoulders. It now held a leaning stack of pillboxes, trays of broken flasks, half-dissected remnants of small animals. A desk, scarred and sagging and covered with crumpled pieces of paper, took up most of one wall. Before it stood a black-wood chair with deflated cushions.

The apothecary sat for a time, silently studying the cluttered top of his desk. He was old, in his middle fifties or more, small and wizened, bow-legged with the left foot turning slightly outward. In his nightshirt and cap, he looked like a cheap caricature of some medieval physician. But what made the watchman stare at him almost shamelessly was the face. Man thought that he had never in his life seen a face which so much resembled that of a stone gargoyle. The lower jaw jutted forward so far that the bottom lip naturally covered the upper. The nose was crooked downward towards the knot of chin, and the eyes bulged from deep sockets. They were never still, the eyes: they roved restlessly from desk to candle to wall, as if in search of something that had been long since given up for lost.

Man had never met the apothecary before, had never even seen him; but there were few in Westminster who did not know something of the doctor's history.

For Charles Dickinson had not been following the apothecary's trade for long, not quite three years now. In 1700 he had still been a fully qualified and properly licensed physician, well-enough regarded to have been one of those in attendance upon Anne, daughter of James II, and now Queen. He had been known as a sober and judicious man, a doctor not only well-versed in theory, but also more skilled than most in the actual practice of healing.

Then, in July of 1700, the Duke of Gloucester, aged eleven, had fallen sick during his birthday party and rapidly worsened. On Sunday the 28th, Charles Dickinson had been summoned, then Drs Gibbons and Hanns, and finally the renowned John Radcliffe. Blisters were applied, cordial powders and juleps ordered, more blisters. The boy had continued feverish and restless, with some improvement in the morning upon the drawing and running of the blisters. The doctors had begun to congratulate one another, and encouraging reports had been given out to the streets. Yet in the evening the boy had been suddenly taken with a convulsive spasm of breathing, a defect in swallowing, and a frightening loss of response. This had lasted about an hour, during which time the doctors had tried every remedy they could remember, while the pale mother stood looking on. Finally, between twelve and one that night, the boy had died beneath their hands. He had been the only surviving child of thirteen, the last hope.

The other physicians had seen the loss as one of the unhappy inevitabilities in their profession; but Charles Dickinson was said to have felt the Queen's sorrow, and his own dissatisfaction, more keenly. He had soon after defected from the ranks of the College of Physicians, and joined the far less eminent order of the apothecaries – an unheard-of treason. The apothecaries – the 'physician's cooks' – were licensed neither to advise nor to administer, being according to law and practice little more than shopkeepers or specialized grocers. In fact, of course, many of them did much more and for a good enough reason: a man might limp for days after one of the eighty or so physicians in London and Westminster and still not find relief. And if he could finally run one down, his case might be no better: according to the street, the physician was cousin to Balaam's ass and would not speak until he had seen an angel – or two or three. Yet there was an apothecary's shop on nearly every corner, and a man might be cured without being run into the Mint.

Man sat across from the apothecary and thought about the old man's changing his work so late in life. He thought again about John Manneux's offer and about the watch.

Dickinson had brought out a pair of long-stemmed pipes, filled them from a box marked with a death's head, and invited the watchman to take first light from the candle. Soon, the small room was thick with hanging spirals of smoke that seemed to dampen all sound and shut them off from the frenzy of the storm outside.

The gargoyle's mouth opened slowly and spewed smoke.

'Where did you find her, Sir?'

'Towards the deep end of this same street, in an unused space between two dwellings.'

'Any man else about?'

'None, Sir. The night is too wild.'

The apothecary nodded. 'When was this?'

'An half-hour past, no more. I could not think where to take her, until I recalled your sign.'

Again the nod that brought the chin to the open collar of the nightshirt.

'You did well, Sir. Another hour out in this fell storm might well have ended her. As it is, the woman's still in a delirious way, but she'll pass now, I'm certain.' The apothecary tapped the bit of his pipe against his teeth as he fixed his eyes thoughtfully upon a darkened corner.

'How came the lady to be abroad on her own at such an hour as this?' Man asked. Trying not to appear too blunt, he added: 'She does not seem the kind of woman . . .'

'No, no, of course not,' the apothecary quickly agreed. 'She is nothing of the sort. From a few words she mumbled while I was at her – she was slipping in and out, you see – I take it she must have been lying there for some hours before you came upon her. She had, it seems, gone out to take in her husband –' he paused as if he were undecided – 'whom she feared might have run into danger this dark night.'

Man could not be sure, but from the apothecary's hesitating tone the watchman suspected he was leaving some things unsaid.

'Said she anything, Sir, about what was done to her or by what men?'

The other hacked angrily deep in his throat and spat into a shallow pail set beside the desk.

'She's been badly used, that's clear enough. You yourself must know the species of men who infest our streets these days – you more than most, from your work. I should say she's been properly "tumbled", as the running phrase would have it. What's that, then, eh? Turn the dame wrong side upwards and practise whatever indecencies suggest themselves to a brute mind. Raped, of course – repeatedly, I should imagine. And beaten in the face and the body. After that, what these young canters like to call the "burning shame" lay. You do not know it?' He looked closely at the watchman, and Man shook his head. 'That's all to your credit, Sir. 'Tis an abomination scarce to be conceived by any right-minded man. A trick with a candle, kept lit as long as can be, shoved rudely up into the secret recesses of the woman's body. The privy hairs are burnt off at once, of course; and, as with this woman downstairs, the scorching and the blistering extend a good way into the insides. I applied a salve both within and without, one of those based upon a mixture of bark and resins. It should soothe the membranes and ease the running of the sores. I expect there'll be no long hurt done to her, unless we mark that done to her soul, and that is not my province.'

Man looked appreciatively at Charles Dickinson and felt thankful that he had happened to bring the woman here. At the same time, he could not forget the woman who was still lying upon the floor of the ironmonger's shop in Green's Alley.

'Have you not, then, bled the lady, Sir?'

'I administered ground pine for its emmenagogic effects; but the application of venesection or phlebotomy, as well as the leeching or the dry or wet cupping, are best reserved for more caustic inflammations or in the presence of a definitely febrile condition. In any case,' he continued, his anger suddenly showing itself, 'as a lowly apothecary, I am suffered to open a vein only as an aid against the pleurisy. This is characteristic, Sir, of the restricting pronouncements issued forth against us out of Warwick Lane.' He spat again.

Man said nothing, not wanting to add to the apothecary's ill-humour, but Dickinson went on, muttering sourly to himself more than to his guest.

'Enough of our numbers, I won't deny, have foully and loosely covenanted themselves to some wide physicians, the two of them going snips out of the most unreasonable rates. And we've as many mountebanks and quack-salvers in our midst as they do in the College. Yet for my money the unlicensed empiric's a sounder judge of what ails you and what's needed than any proud, clean-fingered abbreviator who rests upon nothing save hearsay report and his arse!'

The apothecary puffed wrathfully on his pipe, his gaunt mouth smacking loudly round the smoke, as if he meant to change the situation by an energetic consumption of tobacco.

Man tapped his own pipe out gently and ground out the ashes with his boot. It was time for him to go.

'Is there anything more, Sir, that I can do? If the woman has told you of the men who abused her, I might keep watch for them in the streets.'

'No, Sir,' the apothecary said, looking almost slyly at the watchman, 'she said nothing of that.'

Man felt a tension between the two of them that he could not identify.

'Then, if the woman is known to you, Sir, perhaps I should stop at her home and notify her husband of her condition.'

Charles Dickinson suddenly looked at the watchman with what might almost have been alarm.

'Oh, I should not think you'd find him at his house even now. She herself had gone crying for him, did she not? By this hour, he's most probably been brought to earth beneath this storm. And, knowing as much of Mr Trippuck's tastes as I do, I doubt not but he's resting now with a smiling bitch upon each of his legs.' A look of disgust twisted the apothecary's features, and he forced a weak laugh. ''Tis the posture I myself have seen him take of a night at the Cock and Bull. Our Mr Trippuck is a man of powerful appetites.'

The apothecary seemed more and more nervous, squirming uncomfortably in his chair, as if he regretted every word he spoke.

'What is this place, then?'

'A hummum, Sir, a warm and a live one. It lies, you know, right up this same Row. 'Tis managed by as rum a duchess as walks in Westminster: Mrs Betty Gierih.' He savoured the sound of the name behind his lower lip, while his sunken eyes took on a far-away look. 'I minister to the girls there at times and see to some other of a man's . . . necessities.'

'I should perhaps seek him there, think you?'

'And he shall not thank you for your trouble, Sir, not this night!' The apothecary's voice was agitated and fearful.

Seeing the watchman's puzzled look, he jumped to his feet. 'But hold, I'm dry. Wait upon me, Sir.' He scrambled to the back of the study and rummaged in a deep box.

He returned with a fat bottle of gin and two porcelain cups. He quickly filled both, emptied his own at a gulp and motioned for Man to do the same, and filled them again. In a very few moments, they were on their third.

The apothecary sat down with a grunt and lifted his scarecrow's eyebrows towards the ceiling.

'Against the arriving storm, Sir! The first's for thirst, the second makes merry, and the third's for pleasure!'

'And *quarta ad insaniam*,' whispered the watchman into his empty cup, but Charles Dickinson did not hear.

Chapter 5

From two of the clock the storm continued, and encreased till five in the morning: and from five, to half-an-hour after six, it blew with the greatest violence: the fury of it was so exceeding great for that particular hour and a half, that if it had not abated as it did, nothing could have stood its violence much longer.

Man stepped out of the quiet of the apothecary's shop into a seething confusion of wind and darkness. The storm was fully upon them now, and the street was alive with a fierce noise and reckless motion. At ground level flowed a constant stream of broken debris, some pieces larger than a man. From the roofs of the houses flew a rattling of tiles and chunks of bricks, splinters of wood and glass. And above, shreds of hurried clouds made the far background of stars wink off and on.

The wind sent the watchman scuttling up the street like a crab, his legs wading through the waves of moving refuse. Man trotted and stumbled, jumped and slid. Within a hundred yards of walking, he felt in his legs the trembling ache that comes from hours of dancing.

Blowing mainly from the south, the wind kept pushing him onwards, but its sudden pauses and circular gusts had him badly off-balance. He tripped over the raised edge of the road and once fell into the noisy, reeking kennel in the centre. His lanthorn knocked painfully against his bruised thigh or clattered loudly over the stones. He could see nothing outside the small circle of his feeble light but an anonymous darkness: he could have been walking up any street in any town.

Man felt light and floating. He knew now that he had drunk far too much of the apothecary's good gin and that too quickly: it was the best he had ever tasted, the kind that went directly to the head rather than the stomach. It kept him reeling, sometimes with a nauseating lurching motion; but at times his drunkenness seemed to help, loosening the movements of his body to fit the wind's. He thought of the story of the drunken farmer who fell from his moving cart and landed unhurt, not knowing that he had fallen.

In the shallow doorway of a mirror-shop the watchman took shelter, trying to get back his breath and clear his thoughts of the storm and the gin. Out of the pressure of the wind, he felt again the hard cold of November, and he tried to beat some feeling back into his arms and chest. When he bent down to replace the stub of candle with a new one from his pocket, he could feel a buzzing surge up behind his nose. As he straightened up, his head seemed to drain itself empty.

Man took out his pipe and pouch, hoping that a strong smoke would help to settle his spinning head. The shreds of tobacco felt prickly to his stiffened fingers. The wind found its way to where he stood and plucked the finer grains out of the bowl.

The watchman shivered with cold and weariness. He felt giddy; his whole body seemed less solid than usual. His forehead burned.

Perhaps he should have taken Constable Burton's advice and spent the night drinking and dozing with the other watchmen in the warmest watch-house. What could one man do in a storm such as this?

The night seemed endless. Too much had happened, and Man had seen too much and not understood.

Isabella Trippuck. He had seen her for only a moment in the uncertain light of his lanthorn, but she looked to be a handsome woman with a gentle expression even in her pain. Not much older than Man himself, probably. But there was something too grave about her face, as if she were too used to suffering, and Man could remember having noticed the tracings of deep lines at the eyes and mouth.

He prodded the tobacco more tightly down into the bowl and stared out across the dark and crashing street. Suddenly, without his wanting to think of it, he began to imagine what had happened to Isabella Trippuck tonight, what the unknown men had done to her. He could feel her fear and pain, hear her begging to be let go and the rough male laughing and grunting. He could smell again the stench of burned hair, and his throat tightened. But, at the same time, he remembered the cold nakedness of the woman's thighs, and he felt confused and ashamed.

Man knelt quickly to light his pipe from the candle, shielding the lanthorn behind his opened coat. The flame warmed his face as he tasted the special flavour of a pipe smoked in the night air. He started to reach into his pocket for the trotter that Dorothy Puncheon had given him, then decided to save it for later.

And the ironmonger's wife. Even now, the watchman did not care to remember the woman's face and head, what had been left of them. Her body had seemed so gaunt and sexless, almost that of an undergrown man, dry and sterile. She must have looked much the same in life as in death, but Man found that he could not imagine Joan Fletcher alive and talking and walking. She must have been a hard and unbending woman, the kind that no man could look upon with pleasure or excitement or wish to touch and hold.

But another woman? Man still felt upset that the tripe-woman in Antelope Alley should have suggested as much. Of such intimacies between one woman and another the watchman knew next to nothing; but, as he thought of the dead woman and Judith Woodman lying awake in the same bed, he experienced a deep disgust and, surprisingly, an odd form of jealousy. Man could never forget how, as a boy running errands in the City for his father, he would come out of Beer Lane, cross Tower Street, and enter Seething Lane, passing by a garishly painted house that was rumoured to specialize in such pleasures. He had always looked sideways at it in fear and wonder, feeling somehow vaguely and unfairly cheated. As far as he knew, the house was still there and still thriving.

He thrust his still-burning pipe back into his pocket and picked up his lanthorn. He felt troubled: he had begun to think again about the widow. He did not care to think about her too much; he distrusted her, and he sensed that she lay somewhere near the centre of what had happened tonight in Green's Alley. Whether she had lied to Man or to the Constable remained to be seen; but she had lied, and she evidently knew Zachary Trippuck well. And the watchman wondered what kind of man would attract the attention of the young widow.

She seemed so small and frail and weak, as if she had been made only to be protected and defended. Standing before him, she had trembled uncontrollably, and Man had felt that he could have crushed her small shoulder with one hand. But had he touched her? He could not remember, and it angered him. But he did remember the close, heavy smell of her waking breath, hot and thick, and the strained pitch of her voice. With such a woman, he thought, a man could do anything, anything . . .

Still weaving and confused, Man stepped out into Channel Row and turned up the street. The wind seemed to have been waiting for him to throw its main strength against his back. As he passed the dark mouth of a side-street, he was startled by the sharp barking of a dog – first one, then another, suddenly a half-dozen of them. They moved into the circle of his light – wild, scrawny animals, mad with hunger, their jaws foaming and their thin coats ruffled into spikes by the wind. The watchman had fought with such strays often enough before to know they would stop at nothing. Quickly, he tore the pig's foot out of his pocket, gave the dogs a smell of it, and threw it as hard as he could into the depths of the alley. He hurried on without daring to look back, silently blessing the generosity of the tripe-woman.

Only the blind, Man decided as he stood before it, could pass by the Cock and Bull bagnio without noticing it. Even tonight, the house boasted a steady light in a stout iron lanthorn, the only one burning in the street. Light showed, too, behind the fastened shutters, and a muffled chorus of voices could be heard within the howling of the wind.

The swinging signboard had no need of words; the clumsily sketched figures of the two animals, engaged in an act that was ludicrously impossible for either, told more than enough. Man smiled wearily to himself, wondering what Michael Wells's criticism of this particular specimen of his art would be.

Even the slowest-witted citizen of Westminster would have little difficulty recognizing the brand of services offered by the Cock and Bull. Many of the bathing and sweating houses were perfectly respectable: the one in Gardiner's Lane which Man visited for his monthly immersion had separate days for men and women and an unmarked back-entrance for the shy. But this house, with its dirty stone and its sagging window-frames, wore a look of neglect and abuse that set it apart from its neighbours. It looked unkempt and savage, like the tufts of lichen topping the stone balls that stood at either side of the door. Man stepped nearer and trained his light upon the ground. The balls were ringed with wet trash: a cracked injection syringe, the remains of a soiled petticoat, an empty bottle of prophylactic medicine. The petticoat humped and moved, and a bloated rat scrambled out and away from the light.

The watchman pinched out his candle and laid his lanthorn and staff in the shadow at the base of the building. This was an official visit, but it would not do to madden the other customers with a show of the marks of his trade. Man had heard too many stories of what had happened to other watchmen when they had stepped into such places alone.

Man steadied himself for a moment against the door. The lightness in his head had given way to a deep aching over his eyes. His skin tingled, and he was surprised to find a cold clamminess under his arms. He was thirsty again.

It took the watchman a full five minutes of pounding and kicking to bring someone to the door. A plain-looking girl who could not have been much over fifteen smiled at him from behind a shielded candle. Man asked to see the mistress of the house. As the girl closed the door behind them, the watchman caught a glimpse of a horse, riderless and terrified, bolting madly up the street ahead of the storm.

The girl led him down a narrow hallway that had none of the heat and dampness that usually filled such bagnios, warping the walls and making the curtains hang limp. The doors to the rooms were closed; from behind two of them came sounds of laughter and excitement. A man's husky murmur, a light slap, a high-pitched giggle, then quiet.

Betty Gierih was in her 'office' – the cold, cramped bedroom at the back of the house in which she had set up an unpainted desk in the corner. Two decades earlier, she had used it to conduct business of another kind, when she had been prettier and more limber. And she still herself entertained the more important clients here: the old friend, the rich shipowner, the powerful alderman or Constable. Her fingers, at least, had not lost their nimbleness and could still extract a gold watch or a fine handkerchief from the deepest pocket without the slightest tremor.

Whenever anyone was impolitic enough to ask Betty Gierih her age, the reply never varied: 'Am, duck, as old as my tongue and a little older than my teeth'. But the effect of the question depended upon the inquirer. If it were a gentleman who appeared to be inclined towards drinking and spending, he would be handed another cup and the talk would be turned towards the value of experience. Should the customer be no better than a common sailor or merchant, Betty Gierih's face would freeze in a brittle leer and the man would quickly find himself alone with the weakest gin and the sleepiest girl. And if the question should come from one of the newer girls, the ignorant miss would soon be informed that there were many other hummums in Westminster that could use her services just as well.

Madam Betty was a heavy, florid, loud and energetic woman, as shrewd in business as she was knowledgeable in what would please and distract a man. She seemed to know nearly every able-bodied man in the town and could remember each of their peculiar preferences and habits, as well as the quality of their possessions. The men spoke of her as if she were a kind aunt or understanding wife. Out of her hearing, the girls called her 'Old Hat'.

The watchman looked up at Betty Gierih as she poured him out a cup of warmed gin. Madam Betty favoured the liberal use of patches which she shifted about daily from cheek to cheek and brow to temple in the hope of finding the perfect pattern. In the shadowed light of the back bedroom, these became cavernous, bottomless, and made her puffed face seem dried and leprous. Man looked away.

Betty Gierih continued talking, pausing only to take in great lungfuls of air, swelling her wide breasts almost out of her tight bodice.

'If it's Z. Trippuck you're after, lad, you've come to the place for it. I can't mind the night now when that man's not crossed the door for a drop or brought Old Horney in for a squeeze. As upright a beard-splitter as walks in Westminster!'

She eased her soft bulk into a chair and extended her fat knees forward until they rubbed against Man's.

'Oh, not that there ain't been the odd night when he's stood out; but the most of us know what he's being at, though none of us dare speak on it.' She winked lewdly and refilled the watchman's cup. 'But even if he's wanting, the other three can more than well enough keep the extra piece of mutton warmed for him. They're all as fast friends as ever cracked rings together. Do you know Zack Trippuck well, then?'

The watchman seemed to hesitate.

'Not perfectly, no. I am closer to his wife.'

Betty Gierih gave a chortle that set her breasts bobbing.

'Well, at least some one man should be!' She reached for the bottle. 'But dry that last drop up, lad. Your face looks to me thirsting for it. We'll all of us be blessed to see the other side of this God's night, though the house you've outside of you now's harder than most in Channel Row.'

She looked appreciatively at the low, soot-blackened ceiling and downed her drink at a gulp. A regular thumping could be heard from the floor above and, farther still, the uninterrupted roaring of the storm.

Madam Betty looked slyly at the watchman, contorting her face into a close resemblance of the figure Man had seen on top of Charles Dickinson's tobacco box.

'Ask me how long, boy, this house and me have stood together. Ask me how long.'

The watchman seemed embarrassed.

'You do not appear to me, Madam, to be—'

'Near on twenty year now!' She emptied the bottle into their cups. 'Twenty year since I come up from Deal with my little sister and found myself drawn into Channel Row. And I don't have the single grudge to make against it all. I may be an old dog at it now, but it still gives me pleasure to pleasure them in their fumbling.'

Her eyes became bleary and her head swayed. She had not slept for more than thirty hours.

'Then if Mr Trippuck is busied with his friends,' said the watchman, beginning to rise, 'or is otherwise engaged, it might be better that I wait for him coming out. Will it be long, do you think, Madam?'

Betty Gierih looked vaguely at Man.

'Do you know Deal, then, lad? 'Tis a rum town with the soundest set of folk you could ever want to set your hand beside. I've late word that Mr Thomas Powell – he's a slop-seller by his trade, but as clean a man as I've ever laid under – and he's now standing as mayor, and a good chance is what I call it. If this blind wind drives up the flocks of ships on to the Goodwin Sands as it's done too many times afore, then it's Tom Powell'll lead the good men of Deal out to pick them off and boat them back into the safe and warm.'

Her voice deepened with emotion and nostalgia, and she seemed to grow more alert.

'Are you well with all of Mr Trippuck's troops, then?'

'No, I am not, Madam. Who is with him now? Would they much resent, do you think, my asking him out?'

Betty Gierih shook her head until the fat beneath her chin wobbled.

'And why should they? It's only Roger Twine and Jack Smith are sporting with him now, and they'd soon as welcome a fourth as he. Especially as tonight they're wanting Robin, and we've the odd girl. Do you know our good boy, Robin?'

'Not at all, Madam.'

The watchman had answered too casually. Madam Betty narrowed her eyes and looked displeased.

'That's odd, that. To know Zachary Trippuck and his kin and not know Robin as well.'

'You must know, Madam,' Man spoke quickly, 'that my contact with Mr Trippuck comes mainly from his day-work as a sack-weaver and not from his night-time business.'

'Oh well, that tells it, then.' The woman relaxed and, as she continued, a look of warm sensuality came into her face, flushing her cheeks almost black in the bad light of the room. 'Now Robin is one you should come to know before any. How that one can keep a rut, coming near past what Trippuck himself can do when he sets his knees to it. Here it was last month or so we'd ourselves a good and loud ballum rancum in the house – a loose-skinned buttock-ball, that is – and young Robin was for doing at what would shame my own hanging sign outside. And the drinking and the singing, the swearing and the laying was enough to heat the walls apart. Not a girl but had an itch in her belly, and not a man but had what to scratch it with. And good Robin was hung out there in the faces of all of them.

What it is has kept him off this night I can't see, unless he's been run round somewhere in this Godamighty wind. You've been out at it, boy, yourself by the tale your face tells. Is it, then, as wild as it pretends?'

'It is, Madam. Much has happened tonight that will not be forgotten.'

The watchman moved about restlessly in his chair. He kept glancing impatiently towards the ceiling, as if to remind the woman of his reason for coming to the Cock and Bull. But Betty Gierih was musing again, rambling from one thought to another in the way that always exasperated her girls and charmed her customers. Her memory and her powers of concentration were not what they had once been. Some whispered that she had been maddened by disease or wearied by senility. Some said she was Irish.

Now she was peering intently at the watchman but not seeing him.

'And if the house should break or poor Robin run afoul of somewhat, what's to come of the piece of cole he's to have in hand for me? Here there lands a wind to shake him loose a round tun of profit, and what can he make of it after the last summer? Any man what can't barely keep up the one trade or the one woman has not the face enough for two. When I think on all I've been led to do for that bouncing jesuit . . .'

Man was not listening. He was massaging his forehead and staring vacantly at Betty Gierih's outspread knees. His cheeks were pale, and a line of sweat had formed across his upper lip. The woman droned on.

The watchman suddenly rose to his feet, holding on to the back of the chair for support.

'If you could now, Madam, take me to Mr Trippuck's private

room, I would be in your debt. The matter is urgent, and I have already stood here too long.'

It seemed to take some seconds for Madam Betty to recognize who was speaking, then she looked up at the watchman with curiosity.

'Are you well, lad? Tell me where it hurts you.' She moved her eyes up and down his body.

Man shook his head from side to side like a tired horse and breathed deeply.

'My own weariness only, Madam,' he said, keeping his eyes away from the woman's broad bosom and randy grin, 'and, of course, the quality of your drink.'

Betty Gierih looked pleased.

'I'll carry you up fast, then.' She lurched drunkenly to her feet and moved forward, pushing her chest against Man's, her old hands reaching for his hips.

The watchman stepped back and dipped his head.

'You may precede me, Madam.'

As she edged past him, a look of confusion and deep loathing came into Man's face, and he followed her at a distance.

On the dark stairs, the watchman climbed behind the wide swaying hips of the proprietress, in the wake of the thick dusty smell of her skirts. Betty Gierih was still talking, muttering lowly to herself.

Near the second-storey landing, Man stumbled and fell to his knees. The woman left him in the dark, and he felt his way to the top with his hands. With every step higher, he seemed to move closer and closer to the wailing of the wind.

The room that was always reserved for the private use of Zachary Trippuck and his friends was at the top of the house directly beneath the crowded set of chimneys that topped the

Cock and Bull. It was a small, square room without windows. It had a single winged table in the centre – cracked and streaked white with splinters – surrounded by half a dozen straight-backed chairs, the legs of each bowing dangerously inwards. A tall bed curtained in a colourless fall of cloth stood against one wall. Another wall was hung with tattered paper-hangings that cost no more than pence per yard, depicting a goggling Solomon and an upended baby about to be cut in half. Near the door was a faded painting of a horse-faced woman with grotesquely inflated breasts.

Tonight, the continuous scraping and shifting of the bricks and tiles overhead could be heard below the close passing of the wind. And seen, in the gentle sagging of the already warped ceiling. It was as if a great weight were being added, pound by pound, to the slope of the roof.

Inside, the room was filled with a choking smoke and the smell of stale liquor and heated bodies. There was no fire other than a single candle on the table, but the room was warm. And even before Man entered, he could hear the barking voices of the men, the tinny giggling of excited girls, and a far-off muted groaning and sighing.

Two men sat at the table. One the watchman had seen before and knew by reputation though not by name: a butcher's helper from Bell Court who was feared for his bullying and for his coarse, violent habits. He was a large, flabby man with all his strength gathered into his knotted forearms. The first finger of his left hand was missing, and the thumb was cut short. A very pale girl sat weaving in his arms, her head thrown back and her throat exposed. The top of her dress was open, and the man had his right hand thrust inside.

Across the table sat a younger man with long curling hair and the innocent, open face of a boy. A crushed black hat lay tilted on his head, his shirt was opened to his stomach, and his hose were fallen over the buckles of his shoes. He seemed to be almost unconscious from drink; he waved an empty cup over his head, and his drenched sleeve slapped into his face. A girl with a huge patch in the centre of her forehead sat next to him and stroked the leg he had stretched across her lap. She looked bored and worked her fingers mechanically up and down the young man's thigh.

The watchman stood beside Betty Gierih and looked about the room for the third man, Zachary Trippuck, and listened to the long moaning of the ceiling. The wind seemed so much closer here, as if the storm were a part of the room itself.

The proprietress introduced him with a bellowing flourish.

'Gentlemen, I have the honour of presenting to you Mr George Man, a bare survivor of this same devil's storm that has kept us all within this night, who desires nothing more than to make himself one of your number for these last few hours afore the lightman's. He calls for a cup and for the bit of a feather and the sure delight of your company.' She stepped towards the girl with the patch. 'Polly, you're to leave off your slow pinching for half a breath and take you down to the rooms and lead up that fine sleeping slut of a Susan for this good Sir. And mind the while you're about it to bring back our best blow-book for to joy these good gentlemen from their hearts' cares.' Bending down over the young fair-haired man, she encircled his neck with her thick arms and set her face close to his. 'And you might tell us, Mr Smith, if you're able, where our straight Zach Trippuck has got himself to. Off to wetten the bottoms of his stockings, is he?'

The young man stared blankly before him at the flaccid breasts hanging close to his nose. His eyes crossed, then he looked up at Madam Betty with a stupid, uncomprehending grin.

The fat butcher's helper jerked his head impatiently at the curtained bed.

'He's at lifting his leg at the time; and a man might be let do his work, by the Lord's bleeding eyes, in his own peace!'

From behind the curtain came a low moan and a rhythmical panting, and the wooden frame of the bed cracked and moved.

Betty Gierih threw back her shoulders and brayed with laughter.

The watchman stood apart. He looked out-of-place and he seemed to feel it. He studied the ridiculous paintings on the walls, and his smile looked as tired as the colours in the paper-hangings. He lifted his head towards the ceiling, then glanced at the curtained bed and frowned: the bottom of a man's foot stuck out awkwardly from beneath a corner of the drape. It scrambled for a hold, was braced for a moment, slipped, and disappeared. Man kept staring at the place where it had been, as Madam Betty's bantering voice rang through the room.

When the girl Polly came back into the room, the watchman moved even further away from the table to make way for her. She was followed by the plain girl who had greeted Man at the door and led him down the hall to Madam Betty's room. Slight in build and unaffected, she was dressed – unlike the others with their loosened, garish costumes – in a simple smock that looked as though it had been brought in from the country. Susan walked uncertainly into the room, coughed at the smoke, and turned shyly towards the watchman.

The harsh voice of Madam Betty came between them.

'Now 'tis yours, Susan my pet, to take this young gentleman up and trot him about in your hand a good while until our brave Mr Trippuck sees himself ready to withdraw from his place. And mind you now: none of your pocky half-baking with this one! He's our friend's friend.' Turning to Roger Twine, who had his face buried in the pale girl's neck, the proprietress added: 'Now I'll leave you all to make yourselves known to this gentleman. And where might he sit, then?'

The answer came muffled by the girl's tangled hair.

'Tell him he can sit himself upon his own fine arse, if he has one about him!'

Madame Betty's face set in a wintry smile that did not change as she left the room.

In a quarter of an hour, when she returned and peeked round the edge of the door, her smile became brighter. The men were shouting and swearing, the room was hot with smoke and laughter. The butcher's helper was drinking from a bottle and yelling, while the girl moved restlessly in his lap, her breasts now fully exposed. Young Jack Smith was singing; his companion lolled against his shoulder and was busy carefully curling the man's handkerchief out of his pocket and round her finger. Even the newcomer seemed more at ease: he was refilling his cup steadily and following the conversation with care, although he did not seem to be talking much himself. And, she noticed with concern, he appeared less interested in the girl who sat beside him with her hand in his hair than in looking towards the bed where Zachary – 'stoutest soldier in all of Westminster, that man is' – was still hidden behind the curtains. Madam Betty sighed to herself in puzzlement.

Before she closed the door, she glanced quickly at the weakened ceiling. She was worried. The chimneys had been cheaply and hastily made and of the worst material, and now the wind was tearing across the roof so, shivering the tiles. But surely the storm must begin to die soon; it could not keep on at this fierce pace much longer. If it did, there was no guessing what might fall.

Betty Gierih closed the door and hurried downstairs. The

light of her candle bounced along the wall, carrying with it an old and haggard shadow.

The men and the girls in the upstairs room had forgotten all about the storm.

'But the salve, Mr Twine, when applied directly to the blister—'

The other flushed with anger.

'Nay, Jack, I don't care a whore's farthing for what you prattle on about your doctor's bill or your 'pothecary's mix. There's not but the one right easement for the man what's been to Haddums and brought the dripping milk home sour.'

'And your word for it is, Dr Twine?'

The watchman was trying to light his pipe, but his hand kept missing the bowl and the tallow dripped burning across his fingers.

'Take you off, then,' Roger Twine sat forward in all seriousness, 'to the closest lane at sunrising, when the mothers have sent their girls off to the nearest bake-shop. Then wait you for the youngest and the whitest amongst them.' He closed one eye and pointed a dirty finger at his friend. 'But hear me! She must lie at least the five years off her first flowers. If not, there's no gain by it. Then lend her a ring or a piece of sweetmeat—'

'And if she sets to squirm and cry the holla?'

'Then pass her the hard of your hand and be done with that! Then set yourself to your work, hurry yourself through it, and then carry yourself home a clean man. There's nothing so good for an ache in the breeches, yet I've never heard the least doctor direct you to it. And 'tis more to his shame as well than to yours, I'll warrant.'

The fat man took a long drink and blew out his lips, satisfied with his knowledge. The girls tittered uneasily, and Susan looked down at the floor. Man had finally succeeded in lighting his pipe, and now he smoked it furiously.

An unmistakable sound of disintegrating masonry sweeping across the roof made the watchman slide his chair away from the table. He leaned forward to set down his cup. The muscles in his legs tensed. He looked expectantly at the other men.

Roger Twine was burrowing his large, sweating head between the pale girl's breasts. The other seemed to be thinking. He looked first at the bed, then at the table, then at Man.

'A friend of Zachary, are you?'

The watchman gave him a friendly smile.

'Something less than that, in all truth. But I do know his wife –' looking towards the bed in embarrassment – 'in a small way.'

'Here's another knows the good Isabella,' Jack Smith said, leaning over the table towards his friend and keeping his voice low. He listened for the intimate, regular movement from the bed before he went on. 'What think you, then, Mr Twine, of our fine Mistress Trippuck? Does she still play the maid at home and the willingest cockatrice this end of Westminster without?'

His voice held a note of uncertain bravado, and his smiling face seemed false.

The fat butcher's helper suddenly stopped his drinking and his fondling of the girl in his lap. He glanced worriedly at the closed bed and at the watchman.

'Some things are best left silenced, Sir.'

'Our backward friend here,' said Jack Smith, turning affably towards the watchman, 'has doubtless forgot the too unhappy passing of one Alex Woodman these three years past. Said Woodman was a vile, ungracious lout – an Itchland man, by the smell on him – who fell beneath a stand of unknown sticks in this same street. He departed unmourned by all, yet his killing was a mean act for all that.' The young man moved uncomfortably in his chair, and as he picked up his cup, his hand shook. 'Now there was and yet are some who have heard it halloa'd about that Mistress Trippuck herself was something wiser than she'd need of being about the true authors of that same dark deed. And since that day she'd not let her husband's hand be laid privately upon her for her fear of its leaving a scarlet stain. Such may explain our Zachary's incessant night-work with her that was neither maid nor wife nor widow to the Woodman –' he spoke as if to himself – 'as well as some secret foulness practised in more recent times.'

Jack Smith shook off Polly's hand from his shoulder. He could not meet the watchman's eyes.

'If Mistress Trippuck cares not to honour her husband in his home,' the fat man's voice grumbled, 'then she ought not have the face to play at hot cockles with one of his nearest mates.'

'Is it Robin you're on about again, then? Yet that's not known.'

'Why, 'tis sure as a louse in Pomfret to her man! How else can you answer for her running herself out to his house when good Zachary's away? And Trippuck's not the man to stand easy 'neath the sign of the horn. He's always been one to give back a deal more than he'll take.'

'Yet she's a handsome dame, as we well know now. She might catch at much better bacon than little Robin.'

The pale girl on Roger Twine's lap spoke up suddenly.

'Aye, but he's hot and heavy as the tailor's goose, is our boy Robin. He's more than a handful for any of us. Here, look at this.' She lifted her right breast and showed them a white, crescent-shaped scar underneath.

Man was not looking. Again, he was studying the low ceiling

and straining to hear something hidden in the wind. He had stopped drinking.

A quick series of coughs sounded from the bed. It was followed by a man's gruff voice, the words indistinct, and then by a woman's apologetic whisper.

Susan was falling asleep, nestled against the side of the watchman.

'No, 'tis my thought that Robin'd suit the lady fine enough,' Roger Twine said slowly to his friend. 'Why else stay so often without the house and on such a night?'

'Mayhap for the coin which Zachary himself holds back from her. And her with his creditors shouting to carry the first Constable to her door.'

The fat man wagged his head.

'From Robin, never. He's not got for his own. And this six month he seems run fair off his legs. His pockets hang at low tide after the fouling of that out-of-town lay.'

Jack Smith reluctantly agreed.

'He's all of that, though why he plays it so carefully out of any man's sight is more than I know. Yet to my mind if Robin cannot aid her in the purse, but can comfort her some elsewhere, 'tis all to the good. Mistress Trippuck is one who well deserves more and better than she gets.' His features darkened with emotion. 'Or has got, these late times.'

The ceiling groaned.

The watchman sat forward a bit, as if he wanted to insinuate himself between the other two men, enter into their conversation. He looked preoccupied and unhappy. He gently moved Susan's hand away from his leg.

'This other woman you have made mention of, Mr Smith. It seems that I may know her as well. The widow of the man who was killed. Woodman. Remember? I am not well-acquainted with her, of course, but she seems quite a fine woman to me – in many ways.'

But Jack Smith suddenly screwed his boyish face into a sour expression.

'I fear to say it, Sir, but I do not love that lady much. She is altogether too hard for me: the biting wolf dressed in the lamb's skin. She's one who will greet you in the street with an iron grip upon the pizzle.'

Roger Twine chortled and said: 'She's certain enough kept poor Robin the full two stone under his weight!'

'Is she then,' Man persisted, 'especially close to our friend, Mr Trippuck?'

For the first time, the young man looked at the watchman with a trace of suspicion.

'Is there a meaning behind your asking, Sir?'

Man did not answer. He was looking now over Jack Smith's shoulder at the curtained bed. A long smooth leg, naked to the hip, had suddenly appeared through the opening of the drapes. Gradually, the rest of the girl's body emerged. She was young and pretty and full-breasted, but her face was lined and tired. She moved towards the table with her head down, wiping something off the front of her smock with a man's large handkerchief.

The room filled with laughter and crude joking, gross calls for the man to show himself at once.

Then Zachary Trippuck stepped out, his hands working at the waist of his breeches. He was a tall man, not heavy, but with the sharp shoulders and the long arms that would prove to be surprisingly strong. He was a runner and a fighter. His face had been aged by scars, but the dark eyes still looked careless and quick, almost unreasoning, and the mouth was loose and nervous. He wore almost the exact expression of a medieval representation of Lechery.

His left leg was bent and somewhat shorter than the other, and it gave way slightly as he walked. He laid his right arm about the girl's waist and reached for a cup, surveying the room.

Man thought he now looked even more wild and uncontrollable than he had in the hanging basket in the Royal Cockpit.

Zachary Trippuck's eyes rested upon the watchman.

'Am I to understand, Sir, that you have sought me out?'

Man looked at all of them at once: Roger Twine, his eyes glinting with rheum; the pale girl with her tongue between her teeth; the girl from the bed still dabbing at her chest; Zachary Trippuck, now frowning with mistrust; Polly and Jack Smith with their heads laid together; the quiet Susan, just waking. They were all waiting for Man to speak in the suddenly silent room.

The watchman heard it first, because he had been listening for it during the past hour. The wind had kept battering the roof of the house without stop – uprooting the tiles and sending them skidding off the edge, pushing relentlessly at the stalks of the tall chimneys, loosening the bricks. Again and again, he had heard a distant rustling as of old and brittle paper crumpling: but what he had been listening for was a rustling that did not die away, that grew and deepened into a lengthening tear. And now he heard it.

In one action, Man swung himself up from his chair and hooked his arm about the middle of the girl sitting next to him. His momentum carried them both into an outside corner of the room and sprawled them face down upon the floor. Behind and above him, Man heard a slow and weighty roaring as of a great wind through a hollow. Wood screamed and snapped with the voices of terrified women, stone rumbled and grunted, the air changed to a suffocating fog of smoke and soot and dust. Jagged splinters and cracked tiles and halves of bricks rained down. The whole sky fell, and the cold wind brought in a massive darkness that swelled the room and reached into the farthest corner, sinking Man into the soft hair of the girl beneath him.

Part Two

Chapter 1

*Among these arcana of the sovereign œconomy, the winds
are laid as far back as any. Those ancient men of genius
who rifled nature by the torch-light of reason even to her
very nudities, have been run a-ground in this unknown
channel; the wind has blown out the candle of reason,
and left them all in the dark.*

At five o'clock in the morning, with the worst of the storm
coming on and the moon gone and the stars too far away to
help, the road between Tilbury and London was the darkest
place in all England.

A driver gets to know his road in much the same way that he
knows his wife, only better. As he can recognize pleasure or
anger in the woman's voice in the dark, so he can feel the ease
or the roughness of the road through the rolling of his wheels.
He can hear the turns and the upgrades in the leaning and panting
of his horses. If he has a little light, so much the better; but a
driver with a good memory, smart hands, and able horses should
be able to get along well enough without.

No one knew the road between Tilbury and London better
than Raymond Chambers, and no one owned a surer pair of
hands or a braver team of horses. Yet now, at five o'clock in
the morning, they all counted for nothing.

For now the flying-coach was hopelessly stalled, its right-side wheels run off the edge of the road, and the horses were screaming in desperation and they could not even see one another in the total darkness and the wind was threatening always to tilt the coach over into the dark ditch and God only knew how deep it was and what lay at the bottom. And Raymond Chambers was so busy, what with trying to calm the horses down and checking the damage done to the wheels and running back every minute to reassure his passenger, that for the past half-hour he had completely neglected to spit.

It came to him now as he crouched in the cold high grass, and he laughed silently into the wind and relieved himself of a truly monumental glob. He felt it flung back against the side of his coat, but his hands were too busy wedging flat rocks beneath the wheels to be bothered with trifles. His hands were nearly frozen, but he could still feel the stinging of the raw openings where the rocks had cut. He could almost hear them cracking every time he moved his fingers.

He knew what he needed. He needed a few strong men or more horses or a length of stout wood to pull and lever the coach back up to the road. Or a little light so he could see enough to try to drive the coach out. But as he scrambled up to the wind-scoured road, he thought that what he needed most right now was a long and unhurried smoke.

He felt his way to the side of the coach, opened the door, and climbed in – not to escape from the wind, but to add his own weight to that of his passenger to try to keep the coach from being rolled down into the black ditch.

The girl was terribly cold, her small teeth clicking and her lips bluish. The driver had lit a pocket-candle for her to encourage her against the dark, and now she was trying miserably to warm her hand at its thin flame. Her right hand. The left still wore a glove.

Her eyes were scared, but not hopeless. They seemed to be looking for something in the distance.

'What think you, Mr Chambers? Do we still have hope of continuing on tonight? It is not much farther, is it? To London? I cannot think what will happen, if we do not come there before this day's end.'

Raymond Chambers looked kindly at the young girl, at the twin warm points of light the candle made in her dark brown eyes. He was worried about her. She should not be travelling to London alone; he should not be taking her. He wondered why she wanted so desperately to go and why she needed to be there on the Saturday. He had suspected back in Tilbury that she was not going upon any of her father's business, but suspicion grew slowly in the driver's simple mind, moving as slowly as a tired horse at feed. So he had consented to take her from her home, and here they were.

The man collected his thoughts and collected a deep pool of saliva behind his lower lip. Then he remembered where he sat and swallowed it with regret.

He leaned forward to speak to her. It was not easy for his quiet voice to make itself heard above the keening of the wind.

'Now, Daughter, you're not to fret yourself on our delay. We'll be to see the chimneys of London by the light of the day. The horses and me'll right the wheels soon as the blow lets off summat. Raymond Chambers is a first son of Tilbury Town's whitest hen, and his fortune's not missed him yet.' He set his broad fingertips upon her gloved hand and stroked the back of it gently. 'Nor are you to cry yourself for the wind and the dark or for whatever runners you're to be seeing amongst the trees. The storm's not much beyond a winter's spitefulness; and as for anything what walks upright, I've my old true whip up front, and I can detach the buttons from any man's coat at a two yards' reach.'

He spoke with a special affection, as if he were talking to his own child, awakened from a nightmare.

Pamela Castleton gave him a weak smile and casually moved her gloved hand away from his. The candle set in its holder on the inside wall guttered silently.

'I do not make myself anxious, Sir, for any of that which you have mentioned. I am a country girl and am used to the wildnesses of the weather. And I have a perfect faith in your own steadiness and in your horses and coach.' Her expression tightened with eagerness. 'If I worry myself at all, it is for our coming into the town within the right time. I have made a promise, you see; and a promise writ in pen is a stern one, not to be forgotten or denied.' Her neat small chin gamely tried to look firm, but it quivered.

The rough face of the driver became crafty.

'A promise to your good father, I've no doubt.'

'No, no,' the girl answered too quickly. 'As I have told you, Mr Chambers, my father knows nothing of my going – that is, of where I go and why. The promise I spoke of I made by letter to Mr Defoe himself in secret entreaty for my father. And if we do not see Westminster by the night, I fear me it may be too late. He might be gone, he might not wait.' Her voice shook and she looked down nervously at her hand. 'Mr Defoe, I mean to say. He might have need to remove himself to – somewhere – for business.'

The wind rocked the flying-coach in long, slow swells: they might have been at sea. The wood and leather strained and groaned. The wind brought the complaining of the horses to the driver's ears, or he himself automatically listened for it without thinking. The storm shut them inside the coach as in a shell.

Raymond Chambers was watching the swaying of the candle flame. It seemed to move opposite to the movement of the coach, as if balancing it, but he could not understand why.

The two sat silent for a while. The girl was shaking with cold. The man eased himself out of his coat and draped it over her narrow shoulders. She seemed not to notice.

The driver spoke abruptly, breaking into her thoughts.

'It may be he has quit the town already.'

'What?'

'Your fine Mr Defoe,' he said, raising his voice. 'He may have taken himself off to the country – somewheres in Hackney, as I've heard tell of it. Seems to me that after his late troubles with the Crown, he'd have about as much safety in the streets of London as I've a chance of holding off the tide at Gravesend with my one thumb. And by this hour his pockets must be hanging fair as empty as this same wind. He'd like as have none for his own as for your father and you. 'Tis a wonder you've not been let out of the house at Tilbury, the way that man's fortunes run.' The driver slowly rubbed the palms of his cracked hands together. 'I'm thinking, Missy, that with such help as you're heading to in London, you're like to being left cold in the seeds afore you're out.'

He could not be sure if she heard or not, what with the noise of the wind and her own distraction and weariness. She finally responded, but she did not seem to be talking to him.

'He will not forget, as I have not forgotten. Who could forget the most important day of the year?'

Raymond Chambers sat back in the bucking coach and gave himself up to brooding. He decided that, once he was in London, he need be in no great hurry to return home. The girl might, after all, be wanting someone to drive her back.

* * *

113

There was little enough sleeping in Dartmouth Street during the height of the storm and none at all in the house of Michael Wells, signpainter.

He was restless, moving aimlessly from his room to the hallway to the front windows. He had no fear for his house: he had himself supervised the building of it, and he knew it to be one of the most solid of its kind in Westminster. He felt more worry for the workshop he kept over in Hoop Alley, Shoe Lane. It was in an old and ill-made house that faced directly towards the south-west. He could not bear to lose his stock now, especially with this wind's promising a sudden upsurge in his trade. From what he could hear of the havoc outside, he hoped to see enough demand to keep his workers busy for the next twelvemonth at least.

What kept him grumbling about the house tonight was his concern for his only daughter, Sarah. She was nineteen now – a good solid girl, as true as a lathe, who plied a steady needle, read and talked better than himself, and showed a deep gentleness that sometimes shamed him. Yet the affront to her honour which she had suffered tonight – which he, it seemed, felt more keenly than she – had served to remind him that she was now a full-grown woman and no longer the little girl who liked to rest her chin upon his knee. She would marry soon, should have married before now. Thinking on it did not only make him feel old – he felt somehow excluded, left out.

The signpainter stood in the cold hallway, absentmindedly filling his pipe. That young watchman, now – he had liked him. A bit rough at the edges perhaps, but that could be smoothed away, planed down. A pity he could not find better work for himself, but that, too, could be mended. He seemed to be a sound young man – honest, brave, dependable. The signpainter would talk to his wife about the watchman again.

As he passed the closed door to the parlour, he heard the voice of his son raised in argument. It was a high, screeching, strengthless voice; after listening to it for a moment, Michael Wells moved towards the staircase a little more slowly than before.

Daniel Wells was angry with his sister.

'Had you not insisted upon staying at your friend's house to such an unlikely hour, the incident need never have occurred. I have too much consciousness of my good standing in this city to hazard it for the sake of a common street-brawl with a nameless scoundrel. It is I – what was that?' A loud blow against the outside of the house took away what little colour was left in his face. 'Oh, the wind. Well, and then you had to tell it to your father, and it moves him so that he sends me out into the streets like the lowest messenger-boy to collar the nearest of the unwashed men who are said to conserve the town's peace. And a particularly coarse specimen he was at that, your favoured watchman.' He ended with a juvenile sneer.

Sarah Wells was tired, but she looked at her older brother with a certain sternness.

'Are you more vexed, Sir, at the man's quick courage or at the slowness of your own?'

The young man chose not to answer, only glowering at his sister with eyebrows that were almost too light in colour to be seen.

'You enjoyed his brief company, then.'

'I did, Sir. He seems one who would naturally think of others before himself. That is rare, these times. I only pray I have not been the cause of running him towards his peril.'

'One of the Watch?' The young man snickered. 'We'll be in the final days of the reign of Queen Dick, before one of that band will be seen running any way but away.'

'It is a difficult and almost thankless work,' the young woman said gently, 'which, when it is wanting, is hardly missed. The need is always there, yet too often the right men cannot be found.' She was looking into the fire, and her face was serious. 'And it should not matter what work a man follows, if he does it honestly and well – should it?'

She looked up towards her brother, but he had turned to peer fearfully out between the shutters at the rising storm.

And upstairs in the smallest bedroom, Hester Wells sat with her sewing in her lap, listening to the wind and to her husband's troubled pacing in the hall and never missing a stitch. She was a broad but lively woman, with a complexion that always exactly matched the colour of the signpainter's favourite ale. She rarely left her room, but she knew everything that happened within the house and much of what happened without. She sat secure and contented, knowing that whatever important decisions were to be made in the family would be hers to make. And Michael Wells had already told her all that she needed to know about the watchman.

In Channel Row, Charles Dickinson was still drinking and still talking.

'Never took a wife myself, you understand, never had me the time nor the will. But if I had, I'd have had one something like that same Mistress Trippuck down the stairs. A clean-limbed lady, she is, clean outside and in. And why any goddamned slobbering street-swine should feel the need to trifle with such a dame that way is outside of my knowledge.' He emptied his cup and refilled it in one easy motion. 'Yet the men'll do whatever comes to them with no thought of the hurt or the shame. They're like that, most of them. Any one of them capable of anything. What was it she babbled then, when she

was full out of herself? Something about the men . . .' He moved
the rim of the cup meditatively across his drooping lower lip.
'Something scarce to be believed by any right mind. Must have
been my ears: not quite up to what they were in King William's
day. Damned Sorrel! I could have told him the horse was too
quick for him. Be two years already this March that's coming.'
He sighed and drank again. 'Well, it's as much as could be
expected, tied to a raving husband like Zachary Trippuck. I've
seen enough of him without his colours to know. Could be his
deformity's made him so; there's something in that. A crooked
body breeds a crooked mind.' The apothecary looked off into
the shadows. 'Or t'other way about as well, what think you?
That one, now, she's supposed by her husband to be sweet on.
You think I don't know him! As perfect a Janus as crawls
through Westminster! A small, mean, sick, spiteful sort of man
who walks meekly behind you the one moment and then on top
of you and over the next. What makes him so, d'y'know? Does
anyone? Don't talk to me of that soft-skinned slug and that
good Dame Trippuck together! Never! Must be other reasons
why she hies herself over to there so often. Mayhap to replace
the money that burns up her man's pockets.' He reached for his
pipe, crammed it full from the death's-head box, and lit it
without looking at the bowl. The candle dripped on to the floor
between his feet. The room was quiet; outside, the wind. 'But
what do you think makes the man – Zachary Trippuck, I mean
– look so darkly upon what his wife's at or with whom, when
he himself's sampled every cut of parsley in the town? What's
sauce for the gander's sauce for the goose, eh? But it may be
he can't see it so – nor any man. It's maybe what lies behind
tonight's work.' The apothecary stroked his crooked chin with
the bit of his pipe. 'Could be that's what moves the other as
well – the one they call "Robin". Both of them, then: maddened

and sour because they were not the first. Need to be the one that cracks the ring – or nothing. And they never forget – the men don't – never. Women, yes. And it's such a very small thing, after all.' His pipe was smoked out. 'But they have to be the first and the last and the only, or they make them pay for it with more blood.'

Charles Dickinson sighed and came slowly to his feet, murmuring 'Best see to her.' He wrapped his nightgown about him and shuffled towards the stairs, the candle bobbing drunkenly in his hand. He stepped down, leaving the room behind him dark and cold and empty.

'Wake, wake up, boy, I have a deed for you.'

It was the gentlest of whispers, but it stirred the boy's eyelids; and the soft hand that stroked him beneath the thin blanket broke his sleep. He squirmed and protested and tried to curl up more closely against the warm back of the Reverend William Derham whose hollow, resonant snoring continued without change.

Judith Woodman ruffled the boy harder.

'I tell you to wake, lad. The night is almost spent, and I have a something that must be done for me at once.'

The room in the Gate House Prison was dark and warm with the heat of bodies. A ghost of a fire glowed dully across the stone floor. The wind was a flat ringing in the chimney. The shivering of a rat was a tiny sound in the corner.

Everyone was sleeping. A watchman lay unconscious near the door. Constable Burton was leaning back in a chair at the side of the fire, his hands cupped over his groin. The ironmonger had slumped to the floor against the back wall and was fidgeting in his sleep as if he had a fever. At times, he jerked and cried out wordlessly, then hid his face again behind his raised fists.

The widow looked suspiciously at the ironmonger, paused, and bent lower over the boy.

'Are you waking or no?' She slapped the cold cheek. 'Damned devil's get! Do I have to fetch a handful of iced water for your black face?'

The boy twitched a heavy blur of hair off his forehead. His face looked wooden with drowsiness.

'What is it? What is it you want of me, Sir?'

If the boy could have seen the woman's mouth more clearly, he would have seen it twisted into a malicious smirk. All he could notice was a stale odour of sweet port.

'Clean the dust from your eyes, Jack Sauce, and listen to me well. I have money that is yours, if you will but carry my word to a place near here.'

Isaac Hervey was fully awake now. He lifted himself with his elbow and peered up at the woman in the dark. His voice was stronger now, and he chose his words more carefully.

'A penny would help me, Madam, to drown my sire's madness at me being out the night through. A penny or two. 'Tis a hard enough night for running messages, what with the whole storm being atop of us and all. Two or three pennies might go to warming my pockets in the cold dark. There's witches ride these nights, they say.'

The woman gazed at the boy shrewdly and almost smiled.

A sudden snort rolled the Reverend on to his back. One hand flailed in the air, delivering a speech. The other fell near the boy's hip.

Judith Woodman shushed the boy needlessly and bent down closer to him until her breath grazed his face.

'Can I trust you, boy, to take my words fast and true, without telling a single other soul either during or after?' Her hand resumed its moving over the small thigh. 'It is a matter that touches me deeply and urgently, and it must be done now or not at all. There is no danger but to me; and if you love me, you must do exactly what I say with all the speed you own. Do you understand me now, and will you do as I direct?'

Isaac Hervey sat up straight. He looked quickly about the room, at the man sleeping next to him, and back to the crouching shadow of the widow. His voice suddenly became very strong.

'With the finest will in the world, Madam, I am yours – for five pennies.'

And he held out his hand.

The woman gave a low laugh and reached into her dress. The metallic sound of falling money sounded unnaturally loud in the quiet room. Constable Burton grunted and shifted his bottom in the chair.

'Come with me without.'

The two crept rapidly to the door. The sudden draught of air chilled the room and fanned the fire alive in the grate, but no one woke.

Outside, by huddling low in the deep doorway, the woman and the boy could just keep themselves out of the reach of the storm. The street was lightless, in motion.

The widow tickled the boy's ear with her lips.

'Do you know your way to Woolstaple Market from here? You do? Good. Now you will follow that way, making for the river, until you find yourself at the foot of Channel Row. Past its corner, on the river's side, you will count the houses at your left until you reach the fourth. There is a signboard – if it hangs still – of an empty sack; but the street will be as dark as the devil's rump, so you will stop at the place where the walk is broken up. The man of the house is one named Zachary Trippuck.'

A panicked screaming filled the street, and a few invisible

pigs squealed by. The woman drew the boy closer.

'Now there will be no lights in the house, I don't doubt, but you will knock and knock on for nothing less than an answer. Do you heed me, boy?' She stopped him from cowering farther into the shelter of his light coat. 'Mr Trippuck himself will very like be in by this hour: no man could keep the streets in this storm. Now when you have his ear, this is what you will say – and mind the words closely: "Madam Woodman desires to meet with you this day at the same time and place at which she met you last night: Broken Cross between the hours of nine and ten." Now repeat it over to me, boy.'

He did so in a steady voice, word for word.

'And if you cannot find him at his house, then take you full up Channel Row to the Cock and Bull hummum which stands near its head. You will find that with the more ease, as it always bears a light. He will be there, I have no fear, and the message is the same.'

'But first, if he is not home,' the boy said innocently, but with a hint of wickedness in his voice, 'ought I not say your words over to his wife?'

The widow stiffened and swore savagely at the boy. Then, after seeming to listen for something in the wind, she moved her body closer to his and began coddling him again.

'I don't think we need, honey, annoy the good Mistress Trippuck overmuch. She knows as much of her man's motions as I know of the stars. Should it be she that opens the door to you, you will tell her only that her husband is called for business and then hurry upon your way. She will doubtless think it but another demand for a bill.' The woman turned her face away. 'And that will serve me, too.'

Now the sheer ferociousness of the wind increased, and the woman and the boy could hide from it no longer. It got into their clothes; it stuffed their ears; it set them dancing with cold. They huddled together to share their warmth, but the woman was too preoccupied – and the boy too sleepy – to notice.

In a minute, there was a sudden slackening off in the wind. The woman might have been waiting for this to send the boy out, but it was only coincidence. She slapped him awake and growled at him.

'Get you gone, then, and be quick! You have your money. And bring back word to me when you've done!'

Isaac Hervey set off into the dark. His long, tapered body slipped effortlessly into the wind like a dolphin's through the waves. If anyone could have heard him, they would have heard him whistling.

Judith Woodman did not watch him go. She turned and ran with small steps towards the room which Constable Burton had assigned to her earlier. Once inside, she went straight to a chair at the side of the cot, wrapped a blanket about her, and sat wakeful and worrying for the dawn.

It could have been the rat's scurrying across his ankles or the quick drop in the temperature of the room that woke the ironmonger with a hard jerk. Or he could have been dreaming of walking Green's Alley at night and of stepping into a deep and hidden hole.

Whatever it was, he woke at once, alert and on his guard. He was lying with his face almost touching the bare stone wall, and his opened eyes saw nothing. He lay perfectly still for a while, then reached out a hand to rub his fingertips against the pockmarked granite, as if he were feeling for a way out.

When he turned himself over and saw the cramped room with the dull fire and the sleeping men, he remembered where he was and why. The expression on his face remained calm and thoughtless. He did not move. In the shadow, the soft whiteness of his skin seemed disembodied and unreal.

But then, after having stared for a long time at the humped figure of the sleeping Constable, the ironmonger suddenly sprang into a half-crouch and sidled noiselessly across the room, keeping his face turned always towards the Constable. At the door, he halted to close his coat about him and to listen to the breathing of the watchman at his feet. Opening and closing the door, blocking the inrush of wind with his body, seemed to take him for ever.

Outside, he thought he could sense a dark shape moving along the prison wall, but he could not be sure. He tried looking at it out of the corner of his eye: nothing. He put his head down and stepped out into the street.

Alan Fletcher threaded his way through the dark mazes of the Broad and Little Sanctuaries with careless ease. He seemed to have something of the watchman's knack for walking the night streets by instinct alone: he found the hidden turning into the nameless alley, he ducked under the lowest signboards and vaulted the widest chasms in the rutted road, he sidestepped the abandoned hand-cart. Even in the high flurry of the storm, he somehow managed to escape the squall of chipped tiles that would have taken his head and the flapping of the broken shutter that would have branded his face with its nails. Only once did he stop, when a rolling wooden bucket entangled itself in his legs and tripped him up; and then he lashed out at it in violent, unthinking anger and stomped it into pieces. The flare-up of anger left him as suddenly as it had come; and he continued on his way, calmly and methodically, as if he were merely going about his usual business.

As he walked, he kept his small body angled forward, but it was not only the persistent thrusting of the wind at his back.

Time and again, he sensed the presence of something ahead of him, something that was moving in the same direction and keeping always out of sight and hearing. He could not know if it were man or beast or blowing debris, if he were following or being led. When he had almost reached his destination, the uneasy sensation left him, or he forgot it in his growing nervousness.

Because when he finally stood before the house, when he finally felt the familiar broken street beneath his feet, a wave of fear and indecision came over him that made him want to turn and run back into the wind. The small of his back felt clammy with sweat, yet his teeth chattered painfully with the cold. It was this that decided him: how often had his wife warned him against catching a chill by sweating in the cold night air? Walking back now would be the most dangerous thing he could do.

He stepped up to the door and knocked – at first timidly, then with more urgency, and finally with a desperate and peevish anger.

No answer. No lights started up behind the crooked shutters. The street seemed empty of life: only the terrifying wind and the perfect darkness. Still no answer.

Alan Fletcher moved his hand towards his pocket – stopped – then raised it to knock again. Again to his pocket – again to the door – no answer.

Eventually he drew from his pocket a large and heavy key. It turned smoothly, and whatever sound it made was lost in the wind. In a moment the ironmonger was standing on the other side of the door and breathing hard.

After calling out first one name, then another, then both together, he began to feel about behind the door for the low hallway table he knew was there. He first found a deep box filled with a bristling material that he recognized by touch. Then he found the table with its candle and tinder-box, and after a minute's fumbling and muted cursing he had a light.

Then he hesitated, but not for long. He knew the house was empty. He had been in it often enough before to know its customary noises and lights and smells. Tonight it seemed bigger than usual and emptier, as if the long wind had cleaned and scoured it out, leaving it open and vulnerable to the ironmonger alone.

Alan Fletcher moved eagerly down the hallway, looking curiously into every corner. There was something excitingly naughty about being alone in another man's house that thrilled him. He climbed the stairs to the upper floor. There was just a chance that they might be sleeping too deeply to have heard his knocking and calling. Or perhaps only the woman of the house, lying alone in bed, uncovered . . .

But the bedroom was empty, the bed neatly made. The ironmonger stood still for a few minutes, listening. He was trying to decide if he should stay or go. He had no right to be here; even with a key to the front door, he had no right to stand alone in another man's bedroom. The thought of what the other would do to him if he returned and found him here made the ironmonger's legs ache with fear.

From downstairs came the hollow sound of a door slamming shut, and the man in the bedroom with a candle in his hand felt a sudden muddiness in his bowels that sickened him. He stood cold and unmoving, straining to hear what he feared most to hear. He heard the rhythmical creaking of wood, soft footsteps, a man's laboured breathing just outside the bedroom door, an approaching rumbling, an angry moan . . .

But the house was silent, except for the wind, and the ironmonger was hearing nothing but his own harsh breathing and pathetic whining. He stared stupidly into the darkness.

He had to leave. At once. What he had come to tell, what he had come to beg, would have to wait. He could arrange everything tomorrow. It would be all right.

As he turned to go, the light of his candle fanned the room and caught something shining on the night-table next to the bed. He walked over to it and picked up a wire necklace set with three polished stones. Strangely-shaped stones, amber in colour, holding the light deeply within them. It was a fairly expensive example of an anodyne necklace – a medicinal amulet that could cure and protect its wearer from a host of ailments. This one was supposed to be especially effective in saving men from the ravages of pox. Alan Fletcher had seen it before.

He had bought it himself in the City last spring. He had worn it for a month or so, then turned it over to the widow in lieu of payment. He did not know what she had planned to do with it; but he knew that wherever it should be now, it should not be here.

The ironmonger sat down hard on the bed and began to mash the necklace in his pudgy fingers. His white face flushed red, and he ground his teeth together savagely. The muscles of his jaw flexed and cramped. He began to rock himself from side to side upon the edge of the bed and to pour the anodyne necklace from hand to hand.

How comes it here, then? How comes it here?

He frowned angrily at the unmatched boards of the floor. He began unconsciously to weigh the stones of the necklace in his hands.

Anger came easily to Alan Fletcher – too easily – but not thought. He had to concentrate, moving the index finger of his right hand through the air as if he were arranging pieces on a chessboard, trying to imagine every potential connection.

The widow gives it to the wife, then? As part of the regular loan?

He made a quick erasing motion with his finger in the air.

No, that does not answer.

He sat still for a few minutes. Then a drop of sweat fell from his upper lip on to one of the stones of the necklace.

No, she gives it to him. For money or for love? Either signifies the same. They are close.

The ironmonger looked wildly about the room, searching its darkest corners. His hands were clasped together around the necklace, his hands were thrust between his thighs and his legs were squeezed together, he kept rocking his body as if he hurt somewhere.

The two of them together? The two of them working at me as one? Betraying me?

He lay back upon the bed, still trembling. After ten minutes, the rocking of the wind began to soothe him into drowsiness. He came to a conclusion: what cannot be endured – must be cured.

The ironmonger fell asleep.

He was back in his shop in Green's Alley. It was early morning, and the boy from the coffee-house up the street had just come in and was talking excitedly about the coming storm. He had a letter, he said, for the master of the house. The ironmonger took it with a guilty snatch, gave the boy a penny, and sent him on his way. Mistress Fletcher was upstairs, talking with the widow, but she would be down any moment. The ironmonger tore the letter open with shaking hands, read it, felt the heat rising to his ears. And then the footsteps of his wife, sharp and commanding, began to descend the stairs.

He crumpled letter and envelope into a tight ball and sailed it out among the clutter of iron. Of course, it was the wisest thing to do, the only thing. She came closer. He threw it as far as he could, into the darkest corner. She must not read it. But the footsteps unnerved him so, maddened him, and he was a man of habits. He was looking towards the stairway, and he tossed it away. Or did he? Did he throw it, or – looking the other way – did he automatically stuff it into the leather wallet kept beneath the counter for letters and papers? But then she would have read it later; but then perhaps she did not look into the wallet that day. Perhaps it was still there, the letter; and tomorrow was the coroner's sitting. He could still hear her footsteps coming nearer, knocking upon the hollow wooden steps.

Alan Fletcher woke up, sweating and nauseated. The bedroom was crossed with weak sunlight. And downstairs someone was knocking interminably upon the unlocked front door.

Chapter 2

*About eight o'clock in the morning it ceased so much,
that our fears were also abated, and people began to
peep out of doors; but it is impossible to express the
concern that appeared in every place; the distraction
and fury of the night was visible in the faces of the people,
and every body's first work was to visit and inquire after
friends and relations.*

'And I think it not ill-minded of me to remind all of you here
gathered that what is to be said, determined, and decided within
these walls today must be confined to these same walls and
not bandied about like so many tennis balls from mouth to
mouth and street to street till the commonest waterman knows
more of it than I myself. This is a solemn function to which
we set our hands today and not a child's idle gaming. It is a
truly awesome matter, our sitting thus to question and confirm
the passing of a mortal life – especially, I might add, in such
a horrid and violent manner. We are here, gentlemen, to
discover the truth, or as much of it as our just Lord deigns to
reveal to us. And I, as a properly designated official of this
parish, am here entrusted to guide and direct the earliest
investigations and to forward whatever is discussed among us
to the greater authorities. With these few words, then, let us

begin. Mr Aubrey, you are my second.'

The dry voice of Coroner Fry crackled in the leaden air of the ironmonger's shop like yellowed paper. He was a small boneless man who kept his back painfully straight at all times. When he spoke, he shaped and cut each word as if it were made of hard marble. He never turned his head; if he had to speak to someone at his side, he had a trick of pursing his wrinkled lips forward and curving them around towards his listener. It made him look much like a puzzled baboon.

The Coroner sat now on a stool at the end of the counter and looked importantly from one to the other of the people waiting in the shop. Everyone else was standing, as if the mere act of sitting gave to the Coroner the final proof of the recognized gravity of his position.

Sheriff Aubrey leaned against one wall, an immensely fat man whose shapeless head nestled comfortably upon his terraces of chins. Many people in the past had assumed he had the power to sleep on his feet, and then later found reason to regret it. He was a taciturn man. Some were rumoured to have heard him speak, but they would not swear to it.

Constable Burton swayed restlessly at the head of the covered body, his great thumbs hooked into the waistband of his bulging breeches. He looked bored and unhappy. He had frankly considered Coroner Fry to be an insufferable puppy for as long as the two men had known each other, and the Constable was not about to change his opinion now.

At one side of the shop and towards the front, as if they wanted to dissociate themselves by distance from the inert body, Judith Woodman and the Reverend William Derham stood almost together. The man was still fidgeting nervously, but he seemed to be much more in control of himself than he had been the night before. The woman stood small and concentrated, leaning slightly forward to listen to the droning monologue of the Coroner. At times, she would turn to glance impatiently out the windows into the street.

She looked, too, at the motionless figure of the watchman who stood in the white light of the sun.

Man was only half-listening to the official proceedings. He knew that Coroner Fry had no use for him or for any common hireling of the streets. If Man had not been the first on the scene last night and if Constable Burton had not argued on his behalf this morning, the watchman would not be standing here now. The only look the Coroner had directed towards him had been that of a fussy man who finds an inky smudge on an otherwise immaculate document.

One other man was in the shop. The ironmonger had been the last to arrive, just after the watchman, and he now stood uncertainly at the other end of the counter from the Coroner. By daylight, he seemed even more debilitated and timid, and the jagged collection of his iron appeared always ready to engulf him. The presence of his wife's body, even in gaunt outline beneath the tarpaulin, unsettled him further; and he seemed to need to keep the barrier of the counter between himself and the remains of his wife. He stayed behind the counter and constantly kept glancing behind and under it.

'Then you cannot recall for us, Reverend, the precise time of your coming back last night?'

Man kept his attention directed upon the street outside. There was something about its appearance, the delicate play of half-light and shadow along Green's Alley, that soothed the watchman. The people of the street were beginning to emerge from their homes and shops, their faces lined with worry and amazement, looking from side to side like small helpless animals. Today, for the first time, the children did not come out first: their mothers and fathers held them back, keeping them safe behind them as they scanned the street and sky. The wind was still high enough to fill the narrow street with tumbling debris and an occasional shower of tiles and metal.

Man winced as he touched the tender lump on the back of his head. He had been lucky, considering the wreckage in which he had found himself when he had regained his senses in the Cock and Bull bagnio. The air filled with choking dust and the hysterical screaming of the girls, the men moaning and cursing, Madam Betty fluttering about the ruined room like a demented goose. Roger Twine was dead, his skull split open by a wedge of bricks; Jack Smith's left arm hung at an unnatural angle, and his face had looked paler and younger than ever; the girls had all been badly cut and bruised – the one with bared breasts had sat weeping in the rubble and looking down at the deep lacerations across her chest. Only Man and the girl he had sheltered beneath him had come away whole. For some reason, Zachary Trippuck had left at once, and no one had seen him go.

'At the least, Madam, it would be of great help to us to know if you remarked anything at all uncommon in the look of the street or the shop, when you returned from your meeting with this – ah – gentleman. You entered again by the stairs at the side of the house, as I understand it. But did it not seem unlikely to you that the shop should still stand open and Mistress Fletcher not have retired to her bed? Or did you fall asleep at once, then, upon gaining your own room?'

The watchman allowed the monotonous, desiccated voice of the Coroner to recede into the background. Man felt detached from what was happening in the ironmonger's shop this morning: the inquiry seemed to be taking place in a vacuum, a dreary formality that had no connection with the real people involved or with the dark caked blood on the floor. The witnesses spoke as if they had been rehearsing their parts all night – or so it seemed to Man in his impatience – and Coroner Fry seemed more intent upon scrutinizing his papers for spots of dust than the faces of the people he questioned for signs of subtlety and guile.

Man knew now that the widow could not have met Zachary Trippuck last night, and the watchman had whispered as much to Constable Burton as soon as he had come into the shop this morning. But the Constable had dismissed him with a gruff nod and told him it counted for little. Even Man had to agree: without the word of Zachary Trippuck himself, nothing could be made clear. And Zachary Trippuck could not be found.

The watchman had tried to find him earlier this morning, as soon as he had finished helping to sort out the shambles at the Cock and Bull. He had first called at the apothecary's to look in on Mrs Trippuck; but she was still sleeping, and Charles Dickinson had seemed too fuzzy-headed to talk. He had reluctantly given the watchman directions to Trippuck's house and then had watched him set off down Channel Row, apparently surprised to see Man still on his feet.

And he had found the house with no trouble: a crooked, leaning structure of roughly weathered wood at the sign of the hanging sack in one of the more disreputable streets leading down towards the river. Man had stood ankle-deep in the broken road before the house for a full quarter of an hour, pounding on the door with all his strength. No one had answered. Walking away, Man had noticed a vague movement of shadow behind the upper-floor window, but he finally decided it was nothing more than a trick of the fickle morning light. Man had promised himself that, directly after the Coroner's sitting, he would search out young Jack Smith and ask for his help. That man had struck him as being somewhat less wilfully savage than the others.

Now, as Man idly watched the people of Green's Alley begin to brave the open street, he found himself suddenly thinking about the young woman, Sarah Wells. And he felt sad and somehow guilty when he remembered that, during his hours at the Cock and Bull bath-house, he had not thought of her once.

'And can you tell us, Sir, if you can recognize that one spade as one which belongs here in your shop?'

Man turned to see the Constable picking up a spade that was leaning neatly alongside the others – the one that was now tipped with dried blood. The ironmonger looked at it from across the room and nodded.

'And you can think of no particular man who might have been moved to visit such a horrible death upon your unfortunate wife?'

The watchman strained to hear the hesitating and lifeless voice of the ironmonger, but he could make out no more than a senseless mumble: 'N'mon.'

'What is that, Sir?'

'No man, I said, Sir.' Alan Fletcher's voice seemed to hiccup nervously over the word 'man'.

Coroner Fry actually swivelled his skeletal head a fraction of a degree to the right, and the sudden movement picked up the Constable's eyebrows in surprise.

'More than the one man, then?' The Coroner rapidly batted his almost transparent eyelids. 'It is not a new thought to us, Sir. The good Constable has already suggested laying this foul deed to a marauding troop of unreasonable scourers, and his intimations are customarily acute.'

There was a silence in the shop. The sounds of the street seemed muffled by the dull sagging mood inside. The widow's shoe scuffed quickly across the floor, but she did not move.

The ironmonger's pale fingers played restlessly along the back edge of the counter.

'With all Mr Burton's undoubted expert knowledge of such matters,' Alan Fletcher continued weakly, 'he might miss as well as another.'

Man could see the broad back of the Constable straighten and harden and hear an abrupt brittleness in his voice.

'If thou hast some detailed suspicion in thy mind, Sir, the time to air it would be now.'

Fletcher bowed his head and stared into the top of the counter as if he had never seen it before. He looked sullen and guilty, as if he were angered both at being questioned and at being found out. The watchman was reminded of his own posture as a boy, when his father had caught him sneaking a forbidden flagon of ale.

''Tis not a question of suspicion only, Sir. This is my house, and I know its workings. A house can take its nature from its people, and the people take theirs from the house. And what goes forward in it may be explained or not, I think, without taking ourselves too far without its own walls.'

Man had finally taken a few steps nearer the centre of the shop to hear the ironmonger better. He spoke quietly, drily, with no evident emotion, seeming not to choose his words or even to hear them himself.

Man silently wished that he could move across the shop without attracting the Coroner's disapproval and stand directly in front of the ironmonger. Now the watchman's sense of listless detachment was gone; he felt a gentle stirring of excitement and surprise, as any man is surprised to hear some of his own thoughts spoken by another whom he had all the while supposed to be a fool.

But Coroner Fry would have none of such subtleties.

'I must beg you, Sir, to speak to us more plainly. I have a report to carry back with me, as you must know.'

'I am myself, Sir –' Alan Fletcher stammered, now fidgeting as badly as a boy at sermon – 'a sometime friend to this same Mr Trippuck. I was to make one of a number with himself and two others this last night, had not an unforeseen business called me off.'

'And which business was that, then?'

'Spare and loose iron, Sir, as is usual. Nothing else.'

The watchman was still listening attentively, but he had closed his eyes. He felt suddenly stupid and dull. He was seeing again the signboard that hung outside the shop – the crude sketch of the archer shooting through the iron hoops and the words 'A. Fletcher – Ironmonger'. Of course: Robin, as in Robin Hood, the greatest fletcher of them all.

Man opened his eyes and looked again at the ironmonger. He seemed new to him. The pasty too-soft skin had become a sign of continued dissipation and self-indulgence, the weak eyes had turned sly and untrustworthy, the childish sullenness now appeared as the surliness of a temperamental beast. The watchman felt ashamed of his own ignorance of the people about him.

'And where, Sir, was your company thinking of taking you?' A spark of renewed interest showed in the Coroner's dry face.

'To witness the mains at the Royal Cockpit near the Park. I am assured they continued on to there without me. I yet have not talked with any of them today, but report in the streets tells me that the birds were gaming till well after midnight.'

'But the man may well have taken himself away early.'

'Not if his name be Zachary Trippuck, Sir.' The ironmonger looked smugly at Coroner Fry. 'He is not the man to let pass by him any kind of sporting.'

A movement from the side of the shop. Sheriff Aubrey, who all the time had seemed to be as inert as iron, was now shouldering himself upright to lean his great bulk towards Alan Fletcher.

'Sir.' He spoke slowly, as if the words had just been formed by the ponderous moving of his body. 'Do you think now to blacken the good name and standing of this widow-woman here? I would have you consider that thought again, Sir, for your own caution.'

Judith Woodman suddenly stepped forward. From where the watchman was standing, he could not see her face. Only the small shoulders, the white edge of a closed and shaking hand.

'I am in your debt, Mr Aubrey, for your kind words. A woman alone is an open woman, a waiting victim for the anger and the spite of any passing man. My dear friend who lies here before us now . . .' She gave what the watchman thought was a very theatrical shudder and went on. 'But I do not think I need your protection just here. If Mr Fletcher swears that he knows Mr Trippuck well, that may be true; but I pretend to know him more, and I trust that Zachary Trippuck is not the man to give any of his confidences to whichever unweaned pup that wants them.'

'Really, Madam,' the Coroner began, 'I think this no proper place for personal . . .'

The ironmonger interrupted, his thick lower lip trembling pathetically. He was angry now, and it made him seem both smaller and more misshapen.

'Do you mean, Madam, to question the love of my closest friends?'

The widow had turned now, and the watchman saw a different woman. The soft, strengthless profile had twisted into sharp lines and angles, the muscles of the jaw were knotted, the high chest swelled.

'I question no more than your own mean insolence, Sir.'

'I have given you damned much, Madam!'

'Of what was none of yours to give, Sir.'

'And you have taken more.'

'No more than any dame might take from any ninny, Sir.'

'This has no place here,' put in the flustered Coroner, but the two of them were alone in the room now.

'First, Madam, my wife from my side!' the ironmonger's wet lips spat.

'She never lay there, Sir, but to sleep – and even that uncommonly.' Man saw a corner of the widow's mouth curve upward into a cold smile.

The ironmonger was shivering with exasperation. 'For these three years, Madam, I have borne your galling, lisping presence in my house – whispering my wife and aching my purse – and here's a fine enough end on it!' He finished with a flaccid gesture towards the body beneath the tarpaulin.

'You kept your hand, then, upon neither the one nor the other so well,' the widow said quietly.

Coroner Fry had had enough. He rose stiffly to his feet – an unheard-of action during such proceedings – although he was careful not to move himself between the two combatants. He nodded officially at the widow and turned towards Alan Fletcher.

'Will you favour us now, Sir, with the English of what you say?'

The ironmonger's face was blotched with red.

'It is this only, Sir: this woman has stood these years in my lost wife's house, poisoning the air with an affection for her that was as unnatural as it was obscene and turning her mind and body away from her lawful husband. And even that does

138

not feed her full, but she must treat me to this final betrayal.'

Man felt suddenly confused. Why 'betrayal'? He sensed that in some way Alan Fletcher was accusing the widow not only of the loss of his wife, but of something else as well – something that was even closer to him than his wife and for which he felt more pain and anger.

'And if she may not prove herself alibi last night,' Fletcher said more calmly, 'what was she at, alone in the house with none person other than my dear dame?'

Later in the day, when Man had more time to look back at the developing scene of the Coroner's sitting in the ironmonger's shop, he was to wonder what might have followed Alan Fletcher's challenging question. Judith Woodman might have taunted the ironmonger into a true rage or thrown herself bodily at him, her little predatory fingers flying towards his dismal face. Or Sheriff Aubrey might have roused himself from his sloth once more to upbraid the ironmonger for his inexcusable treatment of a gracious and defenceless lady. Coroner Fry might have regained control of the sitting, asserting his widely recognized and esteemed importance in the parish. Man himself might have found the daring to question Fletcher and the widow directly in an effort to learn more about what each was thinking and feeling. Or the Reverend William Derham, who had begun to swivel his head back and forth like a worried bird, might have added a new tone to the scene by fainting outright.

But none of these intriguing possibilities was allowed, because Constable Burton – with the impatient energy of a careful gardener plucking at a stubborn weed – bent over and flung back the top half of the soiled tarpaulin, revealing the sickeningly mutilated head of Joan Fletcher.

'By all that's good or by the good God damned, will ye all of you hold off for a breath from thine airy chountering and look with both eyes at the lying of this sad maid here?' His voice was rough and strong, and it filled the shop. 'Here's one who hath been used as meanly as may be, felled in her own home with no more thinking than a man gives a starved dog in the kennel. She walked here but yesterday – breathed here, talked here – but now she's no today and none of the tomorrows that should have been hers to have. She's dead – dead as bone – and someone'll need be made to answer for it!' He pointed dramatically at the ruined face, at the inhuman features caked with blood and brain, but no one had the strength to look. 'Now here ye stand, wronging each other upon each other unusefully, when the poor dumb woman herself can tell us more than we need to know. Look on her, then, look on her and satisfy yourselves all out!'

The Constable paused and set his hands on his hips. No one spoke or moved. Man could hear the wind still searching for cracks in the wood of the house. In the shop, the air was thin and grey as if from constant friction against the dull iron.

'Dost see thy wife full well, Sir?' he appealed to the melancholy ironmonger. 'Doth she bleed still? Doth the blood start up again and flow on without stop? Murder will out, Sir, and it outs all times with the blood. I hope to know something more of such work than thou, Mr Fletcher; and I can tell thee that ne'er hath been nor ne'er shall be a body killed and cold that fails to stream anew in the company of the guilty hand. Nay, Sir, thou'lt see more times the poor dead stand half-alive again, wailing and signalling the murderer for all to see. I've seen the same myself, more occasions than thou couldst number! Trust upon it, Sir, that if any man or woman here today could be rightly charged with this dark sin, the Lord would not be behind in wetting this very floor beneath us with the reddest, most steaming blood. Believe it, Sir!'

The effect of Constable Burton's words was immediate. The Coroner quickly mumbled something about concluding the investigation at a more suitable time, Sheriff Aubrey began walking woodenly towards the front door, the Constable respectfully replaced the tarpaulin. The Reverend sighed deeply, and the rigid lines of Judith Woodman's body relaxed. Even the ironmonger, staring down at his hands clasped before him, seemed suddenly relieved of a great burden.

Man was still standing near the window, feeling the abrupt easing of the tension in the shop. He did not really suppose that any of the others had believed the Constable's words: the magical accusation by the corpse's blood was an old superstition that was now more credited in theory than in practice. No, it was the cruel reality of the naked wounds that had changed everything. They would agree to anything, hurry everything along, to avoid standing another moment in the presence of that unendurable sight.

The watchman hung back, letting the others trickle out of the shop before him. He was pretending to look carelessly out into the crowding street, while all the time straining his eyes towards the rear until the muscles ached. He wanted to see what Alan Fletcher was going to do now.

The ironmonger waited until all backs were turned towards him; then he bent swiftly behind the counter and came up with what looked to be a leather wallet stuffed full with papers and envelopes. He thumbed through these in a moment, put the wallet back behind the counter, and straightened up. He was smiling.

Man was in such a hurry to leave the house before the ironmonger that he stepped over a crumpled ball of paper, lying hidden among the mounds of iron, without noticing it.

In Green's Alley the women were rushing fearfully to market, their men were smoking and gossiping in doorways, their children were screaming in play. A tired horse stood yellowing the roadway, the still-strong wind fanning the hot urine into spray. There was a reckless blowing freshness in the sharp air and an unsteady light that made even this narrow and dingy street appear suddenly stripped open.

Already the people of Westminster had managed to come to terms with the storm and its aftermath. The inhabitants of Green's Alley would not be put off their daily routines and swelled the street with their customary cries and noises of business. The cooper leaned out through a jagged hole in his window and twanged a brazen call on the bottom of a brass kettle; the misplaced sow-gelder sounded his horn with the arm that hung in a rope sling; the cardmatch-vendor and the pastry-man balanced their trays in the lift of the wind. A growing press of people surrounded the buyer of broken glass and brick-dust, and the man with the long leather pouch on his shoulder stopped at every door to cry for chairs to mend. Slogging through a mire of garbage, the seller of washballs continued to holler, 'Powder! Powder-Watt!' and the sarcastic bellows-mender swung open fractured shutters to sing, 'Work here! Work if I had it!'

The watchman stood undecided in front of the ironmonger's shop. His three superiors conferred briefly in the middle of the road, then motioned Judith Woodman and Alan Fletcher to accompany them back to the Gate House Prison. The Reverend William Derham, who was officially regarded as something of a dispensable adornment to the proceedings, was cordially sent upon his way. Man was ignored.

The watchman hurried up Green's Alley, and in a moment he had overtaken the speedy Reverend and fallen into step beside him.

'A sad business, Sir, for all of us.'

The Reverend William Derham reluctantly forced his eyes away from examining the troubled skies.

'What? Yes, to be sure. But who . . . ? Ah, of course, the good watchman! Well, yes, the storm has wrought extraordinary damages, there's no denying that.'

Man almost smiled at the sight of the Reverend's innocent good-natured face.

'Yet the tragic loss that Mr Fletcher has suffered must be something that touches you, Sir, most particularly.'

'Oh, that, yes, unforgettable, absolutely unforgivable.' Mr Derham seemed to be weighing something in his hand. 'But the poor woman's pain must have been minimal; she must have come to her death instantaneously, don't you think? I mean to say, when the cephalic cavity is so grossly and rapaciously violated, the stilling of the sentient principle in the brain must be all but immediate. No pain, no; I am sure she felt no pain.'

Remembering the erased features of Joan Fletcher, Man could not agree, but he declined to say so.

'In such times as these, Sir, I pity the surviving something more even than the dead. Mr Fletcher has had the better half of him struck off.'

'Yes, there is that to be considered, I suppose,' the Reverend answered, though a note of doubt seemed to linger in his honest voice. 'Mr Fletcher is a – how to say it? – a man of some obvious delicacy of parts. Of course, I do not know the man at all, you must understand. These few days only. But he stands before me now as one who is in the unhappy possession of – I don't know really – of a somewhat unnatural weakness of spirit.'

The two men had reached the upper portion of Green's Alley. The watchman had been walking slowly, slowing the other's clerical briskness and carefully scanning the houses that lined the street as if in search of something. Finally, Man came to an abrupt stop before a crooked, battered building.

'I fear I must leave you here, Sir,' he said, turning towards the Reverend. 'There is something . . .'

'Yet there is that in the sad case of Mr Fletcher,' the Reverend continued, not hearing the watchman and squinting again towards the moving sky, 'which should perhaps not much amaze us and which fits quite well into the prevailing climate. Something that suggested itself to me soon after I took up lodgings above the shop. I wonder if you know, Sir, the works of Mr Thomas Nashe?'

'I do not, or only imperfectly,' Man answered with little real interest.

'It was in – let me remember it now – in his very singular astrological prognostication for the year fifteen-ninety-one – or two or three or thereabouts. I should very much like to recall it for you.' He screwed up his face in concentration, dislodging his spectacles from one ear with the effort. 'Forgive a vicar's too-erratic memory now, but I should think it was near to this: "Diverse great storms are this year to be feared, especially in houses where the wives do wear the breeches." Yes, I think that comes quite close to it.'

The watchman stepped closer to Derham to make way for a rumbling cart filled with excited chickens. 'You understand the situation in that view, do you, Sir?'

'Yes, well, I have not stopped at the ironmonger's shop for long, but something longer than you, my friend. And I did have the privilege of speaking to and hearing Mrs Fletcher as well as her husband – and, what is more to the point, the two of them together.' He looked at Man with a suddenly meaningful frown.

The two stood silent for a minute, as the filling narrow street jostled and shoved about them. Man felt a new admiration for the Reverend William Derham, and he felt himself even younger than he was.

'You are making to where now, Sir, if I may ask?'

'Oh, off to a fellow Society man's house,' the vicar answered, his face brightening, 'to beg a bed for the next few nights. And then, this afternoon, the men mean to feast me once again at some location called Old Palace Yard – do you know it? But you should, of course. We're to start ourselves at some tavern named Purgatory and then move on to another called Heaven. That seems most appropriate, does it not, for one of my work? Although,' he added as a bemused afterthought, 'I must really pledge myself not to take quite so much drink as I did this last night.'

The watchman smiled at Derham's expression of gentle regret.

'Take greater care, Sir,' Man shouted as the other began to move off, 'not to end at another in that same Yard which is well-named Hell. I know that house myself.'

'Oh, is there now? Well, I shall watch for that one, with all my eyes I shall!'

The Reverend strode off up the road, his face lifted to the clouds again, happily unconscious of a pool of swine that soon engulfed his legs.

Man stood watching him until he was out of sight, then turned to go in.

It was a coffee-house or a tavern or a cook-shop or an inn or something that managed to combine the worst qualities of all of these. It would have had a name – and probably a coarse one – if it had had a signboard. The merchant would stop in here for a quick coffee, thick and scalding as soup; the coal-seller would run in for a warm ale and leave his black fingerprints unnoticed on the door; the underfed boy would be sent in from across the street for a doubtful piece of meat and hurry in past the drunken couple searching for a hard bed to be let by the hour. It was a dark and wretched place with a broken ledge across the front like a frowning brow. It was made for Green's Alley, or the alley was made for it. And it thrived.

The watchman ducked through the low doorway and was met with a wave of smoke and bitter fumes that puckered his nostrils. The single room was lined with long tables and benches and crowded with hoarsely swearing men, some spitting insults at one another and others knocking the ends of their long pipes together. The proprietor – a hairy man from whose single massive eyebrow the front of the house must have been modelled – sat in a square wooden booth at the side of the room, directing the waiters and exchanging moneys with the same permanent scowl.

Man made his way quickly to the back of the shop where a scarred cauldron bubbled over the fire behind a row of soot-darkened coffee-kettles. He had, earlier this morning, sent an eager street-boy from Channel Row to the watchhouse near the Abbey with his staff and his lanthorn and a penny; but even now, marking the easy way he swivelled the upper part of his body from side to side as he walked, few in the room could not guess at his customary trade.

Man sat and smoked and tried to swallow his coffee. He kept his eyes on the proprietor's wooden booth. Most of the hairy man's time was devoted to orders and bills; but, every few minutes or so, someone would walk into the shop, make straight for the booth, give or receive some folded paper, and leave again without drinking anything. And once, after Man had been sweating at the fire for nearly half an hour, a small boy with a bent back came in, carrying an empty sack. The proprietor filled the sack with letters and treated the boy to a short glass of gin before sending him out again.

It was a common enough practice. Most of the coffee-houses, especially in such a poor and self-contained neighbourhood as this one, acted as informal collection points for the post. The surrounding streets were serviced by means of messengers who knew the area minutely, and most people fell into the habit of citing the local coffee-house as their personal address. It was hardly a dependable system and only rarely a consistent one, but it was usually all the people had.

And, this morning in the ironmonger's shop just down the street, Alan Fletcher had seemed to be looking frantically for a letter.

The watchman wondered why. Last night had been a post night, but Man knew that no one could have bothered with such duties at the height of the storm. And he was suddenly very anxious to learn as much as he could about the character and the actions of Alan Fletcher. Now Man knew that the ironmonger wore one face in the shop by day and quite another, more vicious one in the streets by night. And this morning, at the Coroner's sitting, Fletcher's anger and spite against the widow had been breathtaking. How much more was there to be discovered about the soft, deceptive ironmonger? Perhaps Judith Woodman, whatever her guilt, had not acted entirely alone.

When the boy with the bent back had finished licking his glass clean, he shouldered his loaded sack and made for the door. Man slapped a coin down loudly upon the counter of the wooden booth and caught the boy up in the street.

'Know the ironmonger-man that keeps a shop down this same street? Robin, he's sometimes called.'

The boy's eyes were watery with the cold, and his red-tipped nose trickled down over his drawn lips. He eyed Man with distaste, and his face hardened into an expression which the watchman himself did not feel old enough to attempt.

Man took out a penny and rubbed it against his own chin, hoping to change the boy's mood, but the messenger only started to run away, muttering, 'That's small enough,' in disgust.

A second penny brought him round, reluctantly.

'The cove what's placket's been bunged?'

'You understand me. Called for a letter yesterday, did he?'

'Not him.'

'Ran it into him yourself?'

'No more'n my right work, is it?'

'Where from?'

The boy hesitated, but the coins in the watchman's hand still held his eyes.

'Down Tilbury-way, if it accounts for aught.'

'Man's hand or woman's?'

'Prettier'n yours, at any wager.'

'Didn't happen to catch the sense of it?'

The boy quickly plucked the money from Man's hand, bit his thumb at him, and ran off.

For a long time, the watchman stood musing in the road, while the restless traffic parted and made way for him. He was repeating to himself the name of the town.

Then he set off up Green's Alley at an awkward run, at a speed that had old men wondering worriedly what could be chasing him and proper ladies – or as proper as could be found in that part of town – cursing his mad behaviour under their breaths. Knots of bored street-lads cheered him on.

Up busy King Street the watchman hurried himself faster, his tiredness and bruises forgotten. It was a small thing that he had remembered, but it was enough to keep him as excited and anxious as a young man on his first private visit to a woman's room.

He turned left into George Yard and ran straight towards a plain wooden house that seemed to have fallen accidentally between a chandler's and a barber's. The watchman stepped down and through the door without breaking his quick stride. Few ever came to this door, and the few who did knew there was no use in knocking.

Man moved down a short dark passageway towards the back of the house. A smell as of an old book left out in the rain grew upon him as he walked. By the time he reached the low-ceilinged airless study, he could scarcely breathe.

The room seemed almost to have been constructed out of paper. Books crowded one another off sagging shelves, towered in stacks, leaned in files across the corners. Miscellanies and pamphlets lay scattered everywhere, some of their pages cracked off at the edges or half-torn and hanging out as bookmarks. Fat journals and reviews merged with limp news-sheets to blanket almost all of the floor space with a dirty yellow or grey that shaded the light from the room's one miniature window.

The watchman spoke to a curl of pipesmoke that rose from behind a pile held together by dust and a spiderweb.

'I trust I find you, Mr Wolfe, not in the worst of your health.'

The man who started up and came towards the watchman with his hand outstretched was a tall and fairly heavy man, perhaps only a decade older than his visitor, but ageing much faster. His muscles looked weak from disuse: the posture of his body always reminded Man of a question mark. His face had a washed-out colour, and the eyes that looked out over the spectacles were yellowed. A wrinkled coat hung to his knees, his calves were wrapped in wool, and a chipped toenail stuck out of one of the mouse-eaten felt slippers.

He took the watchman's hand in a strong grip, but then moved it to his face and pressed his cheek against the palm. Man was not surprised. Homer Wolfe was a valetudinarian of long standing. His dread was uninterrupted: he had never been injured, but he feared everything; he had never been seriously ill, yet he was always sickening. He got better, or worse, but he never got well. His horror of contracting an incurable disease had, after so many years of melancholy, become an incurable disease.

Man smiled patiently and withdrew his hand. 'I am not the best to judge, my friend. My hand is chilled from the wind. The slightest of fevers, I should say, but nothing more.'

Wolfe gave an automatic nod of satisfaction and led his guest to a chair near his own. A candle stood in a dish on a three-legged table, and he lifted it towards the watchman's marked face.

'What is it, then, that's had you, Sir? They go deep, they do. Might well infect.'

'Nothing, Mr Wolfe, nothing at all. All's on the mend already.' As he spoke, Man glanced uncomfortably at a stand of journals and read a title: *The Night Walker: Or Evening Rambles In Search After Lewd Women*, by J. Dunton.

'There's some pretty enough pieces there,' said Homer Wolfe, following the watchman's eyes, 'but unhappily outdated by this day. And heed the paper. It cuts. Look here.'

He held out a smudged finger, and Man pretended to be able to see something.

'I do not mean, Sir –' Man spoke rapidly – 'to speed our talk unkindly; but I have just this moment recalled something that I wish to make sure with your help. You are, I think, the one gentleman in Westminster who can do so.'

'However I might help, of course.'

The watchman folded his hands together, set his elbows upon his knees, and rested his chin upon his thumbs.

'You know, I would imagine, of the late difficulties of the man named Daniel Foe – he who is these times called "de Foe" by himself and some others.'

'And who could not, friend? He is but this month begun to see the other side of them. You have read the pamphlet in question, I know.'

'Aye, at the first; but it is with the man himself I bother me now – with his work in business, not in print.'

'So should he have done as well, and now 'tis to his pain.'

The conversation was suddenly broken by an exploding, wet cough. Homer Wolfe hacked noisily and spat into a stiffened square of burlap. He brought it nearer to the light and prodded at the coagulated phlegm with his finger, moaning unhappily all the while, until he remembered the cut and then wiped the finger frantically on his filthy coat.

'There's red in that,' he murmured, looking wistfully at the square of burlap, 'or I'm a dead man.'

'This de Foe,' resumed the watchman less patiently, 'is said to entertain certain large interests outside the town. It may be one of these that concerns me now. You remember that it was in January that a warrant was prayed against him that led to his eventual arrest and imprisonment?'

'I do, Sir. And one of the surprisingest pilloryings that London has witnessed in its day.'

Man smiled in recollection. 'That, too. But I seem to mind some announcement of the warranting in, I think it was, the *London Gazette* of the time. Would you have some of those sheets by you still, do you know?'

'As easy done as said, my friend.'

Homer Wolfe stood up and strode over to a corner of the room with all the certainty of a man feeling for his own limbs in the dark. He began to burrow and the paper flew with the crackling sound of a sheltered fire. Man heard the tinny scurrying of a rat's feet.

The watchman had just started to skim through the works of J. Dunton, when Wolfe returned with the issue for the eleventh of January. This contained a small announcement, dated the previous day, of a reward for the apprehension of one 'Daniel de Fooe' or 'Daniel Fooe'. There were few particulars.

'I recognize this,' said Man. 'But a somewhat fuller accounting of the man I think there was. Perhaps a few days after.'

Wolfe nodded, twitched his stomach convulsively – a favourite habit – and dived into a wholly opposite part of the room. He surfaced in a moment with a copy of the news-sheet for the fourteenth.

Man angled the page to catch the light and read of 'Daniel de Foe *alias* de Fooe':

He is a middle sized spare man, about forty years old, of a brown complexion and dark-brown hair, but wears a wig, a hooked nose, a sharp chin, grey eyes, and a large mole near his mouth, was born in London, and for many years was a hose-factor in Freeman's Yard in Cornhill, and now is the owner of the brick and pantile works near Tilbury.

The watchman sat with his friend a while longer, listening to his intricate complaints and discussing the passing storm. Man wondered again about the life of the strange recluse. Homer Wolfe followed no visible profession or trade and courted none of the favours of the great, yet he seemed always to have enough coin to secure himself a copy of virtually everything printed in London and Westminster and a fair number of others from abroad. A few rumoured it about that he was connected to one of the wealthiest families in England; but many more whispered that he acted as a secret gatherer of information for the government, first for King William and now for Queen Anne. Man himself inclined towards the latter theory: scattered about the base of his friend's chair were many books and pamphlets concerning the present political troubles and an equal number which Man guessed to be in French and Spanish. And whenever the watchman shifted the talk towards the currently developing war, Homer Wolfe would be seized by a protracted bout of convenient coughing that returned them at once to the subject of health.

As Man was thanking his friend for the loan of the *Gazette*, Homer Wolfe pressed him to take as well the journal of J. Dunton which had caught his eye. Man accepted, but he could feel his cheeks burning until they were almost as hot as his friend's, which both men now had to agree were definitely inflamed.

Outside in the cold scoured air, Man suddenly realized how hungry he was and set off to look for the nearest tavern. He felt more confident now, as if he were inching closer to an understanding of Alan Fletcher – his character and his activities, both public and private – which must lead to a deeper understanding of the ugly death of his wife.

Last night had been a night of great confusion, but the watchman thought he could remember the Reverend's chaotic words well enough to recall some kind of linking between Alan Fletcher and Mr Defoe. And if the ironmonger did share that man's friendship, he might also share some of his troubles – troubles that somehow were centred upon the distant town of Tilbury.

Chapter 3

. . . and about three o'clock in the afternoon, the next day, being Saturday, it encreased again, and we were in a fresh consternation, lest it should return with the same violence. At four it blew an extreme storm, with sudden gusts as violent as any time of the night; but as it came with a great black cloud, and some thunder, it brought a hasty shower of rain which allayed the storm; so that in a quarter of an hour it went off, and only continued blowing as before.

The interview was going badly, and it was mostly Man's fault. He should not have begun it as he had, and certainly not in such a place as this. And he could not even tell himself clearly why he had chosen it.

He was seated at the back end of one of the two long tables that ran parallel down the length of the narrow room. The benches at the sides were so crowded that a thick block of wood had had to be set upended to serve Man as a stool. It was rough and unsteady, and it came to something of a point. And the watchman had had to pay extra for it.

He was in a nameless cellar-tavern in the Little Almonry some few streets behind the Gate House Prison. It was easily one of the dingiest and most degenerate public-houses in all of

Westminster and London. It sank beneath the weight of a private almshouse that was famous only for its questionable policies and its unexplained deaths. A cold stairwell with steps cut out of the black earth was the tavern's only entrance and exit, two wooden gratings at street level and choked with cobwebs its only ventilation. The light in the room came from too few smoking candles, and the warmth depended upon the number and the anger or the drunkenness of the customers.

Due to its location, the tavern was a meeting-place for every variety of beggar from the old honest woman with toy-sized hands that could not wield a needle to the neat and proud gentleman who kept a fine house and carriage from the squads of boys he sent out every morning to go begging naked in the streets. Here the artists gathered to trim the edges of coins and salvage the silver for gin; the angler and the receiver met here to sell and buy and make plans for tomorrow; and the rum divers felt freer here than elsewhere to pool openly on the table their day's booty of handkerchiefs and pocketbooks. They all represented the invisible population of Westminster, men and women and children as transparent a part of the streets as the dust itself: and for this reason they felt themselves most at home in the Almonry's lowest cellar-tavern, hidden out of sight beneath the surface of the town.

Man had just succeeded in persuading the tavern's sole waiter – a stunted man with a twisted lip whose sour smell lingered long after him – to bring him a burning straw to light his pipe. Now the watchman sat with one elbow propped upon the table and puffed busily at the crackling tobacco, adding his contribution to the already stifling atmosphere. His blue-grey smoke hovered and sank and coagulated in the lap of the woman who was sitting still-backed at the end of one of the benches.

Judith Woodman did not want to be here, did not belong

here. It showed in the way she tilted her head back for breath, in the way she dabbed at her pinched nose with the corner of a spotless handkerchief and tried primly to ignore the slobbering of a drunken beggar beside her. Man had seen her quail when the boy had first led her down into the stench and the noise of the room; and as she had come forward to submerge herself in its squalor, he had seen her retreat more deeply into herself at every step. She had at last consented to sit, but she had refused the watchman's offer of food and drink and since then had not spoken a word.

Man had not planned this interview. After eating and walking leisurely and thoughtfully down Long Ditch, he had come upon the boy, Isaac Hervey, lounging before the Gate House Prison. It had taken only a little coaxing and one or two mild threats to get the boy to tell his story: how last night the widow had sent him with a message to the house of Zachary Trippuck; how he had lost his way until dawn, only to find the house empty; and how he had just been in to see the woman, after waiting for her all morning. Isaac Hervey had opened his collar and shown the watchman the hot red welt on his neck that was the sign of the widow's displeasure. It was that mark, more than anything else, that had made Man think to lure the woman out of the Constable's room and into the impersonal roar of the cellar-tavern. Perhaps this was why the watchman had chosen the place: this was his element, his home ground, not hers.

Now Man tilted his makeshift stool towards her and mumbled a few words of facile apology, trying to add to his voice a confidence which he did not feel. In the cramped space at the end of the table, the knob of his knee came into contact with the widow's.

Judith Woodman finally bent forward to speak, but she kept her eyes focused coldly above the watchman's head.

'I can assure you, Sir, that Mr Burton shall hear something of your vile game soon enough. To steal a respectable and widowed woman into this unclean circle is criminal enough; but to meanly deceive her with another man's name – that, Sir, will not be endured! And I can tell you that Mr Trippuck himself will be far from pleased to hear that his name has been taken up and worn by another like any common beaver found in the street. He is not one to treat such boyish presumptuousness lightly.'

Her voice was cool and brittle as frost in the heat of the tavern; but Man could feel her breath sweeping against his mouth, and it smelled stale and thick with a sudden warmth that was as intimate as nakedness. He saw the soft fullness of the lips and the red point of the tongue, and he noticed for the first time the upper front tooth that was chipped half away. Man sat back.

'I look for a talk with that same gentleman myself, Madam, but he appears to have quit the streets. I had thought that you, perhaps, could tell me where he might be keeping himself today.'

'I know nothing of his movements – today – though I know him closely.'

'As you have said more than once, Madam. And his wife?'

'Whose?'

Man saw the broken tooth prick at the lower lip.

'Mr Trippuck's, of course,' the watchman said smoothly. 'He has a wife, you must know. Isabella. A fine and a quiet woman, as I have heard, gentle as a doe and with a singular sort of beauty in her face and form.'

Man had spoken with honest feeling, but Judith Woodman suddenly bristled with indignation.

'A rabbit, Sir! No more nor less. Nothing greater than a halfp'worth of dry niggle for a man the like of Zachary Trippuck!'

'Yet sweet enough, it seems, for the tastes of a man like Robin.'

She laughed, but it sounded forced to Man. 'I wonder much that you think that, Sir. You understand Mr Fletcher something more than I had guessed and something less than you ought. He's a wild enough rider, true – not unlike my late husband who led him to it – but he favours those who are younger and more maiden than the Trippuck woman, or those who can act it. I should say she lies somewhat too far from her greens for him, and for her own dear husband as well.'

'Then why is it said, Madam, that 'tis what the man himself both thinks and fears?'

'Which man, then? The ironmonger?'

'Nay, the other.'

Man was trying his best to appear casual, almost unconcerned with the direction in which the conversation was moving. He tapped the still-burning dottle from his pipe on to the table, refilled the pipe quickly, and slid the embers back into the bowl to light the fresh tobacco. He finished just in time to be momentarily distracted by the shrug that lifted the widow's round breasts beneath the white muslin tucker.

'Mr Trippuck—' the widow paused and moved her mouth slackly as if she were tasting the name – 'Mr Trippuck believes what is perhaps best for him to believe. If he sees his dame in the ironmonger's bed, there's no damage done to any for that. It may but help to centre his interests elsewhere.' She picked reflectively at a small black patch set deeply in the dimple in her chin: Man was sure she had not been wearing it last night.

'So 'tis your supporting the woman with loans that keeps her so often at the shop, is it?'

'Who was it told you that, Sir?'

'None need tell me, Madam, what lies ready to be guessed.

Mr Trippuck beggars his wife for his own delight, she must needs find the coin somewhere, and Robin has hardly enough kept secreted from his own wife to please himself. I should suppose that Mrs Fletcher herself was not a giving woman.'

'She might have lent another a penny to raise him from the dead, if she could have been first assured of being returned two.' The widow looked down at Man. 'Yet she made no great mistake there, I think: 'tis a child's game, Sir, to run after any joys that cannot be sometime made to pay.'

'And it pays you, then, to keep Isabella Trippuck coming to you for aid? The further her husband strays from her side, the nearer he lies to yours. 'Tis a fine puppet-play, Madam, if the man should never feel the strings.'

The woman made no effort to answer, but stared icily at the watchman. Then she abruptly straightened her back, scanning the filled room and busying her hands as people do when they are making ready to leave.

Man struggled desperately to think of something to say that would stop her from leaving. He spoke as if by reflex, almost without hearing his own words.

'And the ironmonger, Madam. Does he trade often at your shop as well?'

Judith Woodman stopped gathering her skirts together, and for the first time Man saw her smooth face crease with uncertainty and worry.

'Your meaning, Sir?'

Man lifted his shoulders. 'Well, I fancy that Mr Fletcher must stand always in need of coin: the pleasures of the night come dear.'

'Yet he is rumoured to have other dealings, both in town and out, of which his wife suspected nothing.'

'I have heard that, too. But they are said to have fallen away badly of late. And you have made mention, Madam, of Joan Fletcher. Did you know her well?' Man could not prevent the soft tone of sarcasm from entering his voice.

The widow smiled wickedly. 'Not half as well as the ironmonger himself pretends to believe – but, yes, fully well enough. You did not know her alive, did you, Sir?'

'Not at all, no.'

'Hardly a right woman, by any man's measure. Cold and frowning and practical, with a mind turned towards naught save money and money. Not the smallest part on her for poor Robin to warm his hands on. She'd sprung from a wretched family, had to make a way for herself as a girl—' the widow hesitated and looked meaningfully at Man – 'as best she could. Then when she snared the husband and the shop at the once, she set herself among the iron with a very vengeance. 'Twas her hand that lay upon the business, of course. Much too much for the Fletcher, she was. He'd lost the reins before he fair got mounted.'

'She could not have known of his gaming?'

'Sir,' the widow answered indulgently, 'the man still lives, does he not? And he's not, I think, been gelded in fact as well as in practice. Joan Fletcher was a perfect woman: the only one she knew. She could not stand any sort of viciousness in another. Some of them are like that – after.'

Man did not understand the last part of what Judith Woodman had said, but he was too busy trying to follow his own confused thoughts to bother with it now.

'And yet you yourself, Madam, might easily have told the woman all. And you told her nothing.' Man was staring towards the back of the room. 'Do you love the ironmonger so much?'

What had caught the watchman's attention was a small, low table set beside the door leading to the kitchen. On it stood three straight stacks of flat dishes, each stack containing what looked to be twenty or thirty dishes. The piles were freestanding, but formed with an almost geometrical precision. As Man watched, the waiter came to add another handful to the middle tower: he balanced and aligned them with surprising carefulness. His apron was blacker than the earthen floor, he had not been shaved this month, and he was notorious for tossing the lees of tankards back over either shoulder; yet he had grown into the habit of arranging the dishes into a model of neatness, and now he did it without thinking.

For some reason, Man suddenly remembered the spades.

Judith Woodman had pulled herself up at the watchman's question, as if she had felt her pride being physically attacked. She was angry again, but now it was a colder anger, an anger more calculated and triumphant.

'If I disclosed nothing, Sir, it was from a care neither for Mr Fletcher himself nor for her that now lies dead. The woman, true, often exerted herself specially to please me; yet had she little enough to give me worth my while. As for him that some call "Robin", he is and has been for long a weak and grudging and diseaseful portion of a man who faults all others before himself and dares do by night what he dare not own by day – not even to the woman who is meant to share his bed! Never sated and therefore never solvent, that's him; as fond a bumfiddler as ever let his hair grow through his hood to the emptying of his pockets!' Man could feel the hot breath against his face and a fine spray from the lips. 'You yourself were present in the shop this morning, Sir; you have heard the quick wrath of the man. And that's but the skin on it, I assure you. He's one can work himself into a demon in a breath. Him to his play, and the rest of us to suffer him when it comes wrong!'

There was a new intentness in the way the watchman was

now studying the face of Judith Woodman, a new carefulness the woman herself should have noticed. Man moved forward until his clasped hands were almost brushing against the folds of her skirts.

'Then your long silence must have gained you more than the telling. In which ways, Madam?'

Whatever kind of response Man was expecting, he could never have foreseen what the widow did and said next.

The soft and vulnerable womanliness fell from her like a shawl, her features suddenly took on all the wily rapaciousness of a veteran in 'Change Alley, her entire body appeared to crouch. Man was not prepared for such a grotesque transformation; and when, under cover of the table, the woman viciously thrust her hand up between her legs, the watchman felt his own groin cringe.

Her hissing voice was loud enough to startle the nodding beggar sitting beside her. 'All that speaks, Sir, in Westminster and beyond is what you've hanging in your cod! And secrets cost!'

For an insane moment, Man wondered if Judith Woodman had magically changed her sex as well, until he realized that she must carry her purse there for safety.

She was herself again – feminine, proud, yet tractable. The tavern mumbled again with voices and the knocking of cups on tables. Man almost doubted the reality of what he had seen.

For a second time, the woman started to go through the motions of getting ready to go. Then, slowly and thoughtfully, she reached into a hidden pocket and brought out something which she tossed lazily into Man's lap. The anodyne necklace encircled his knee.

'He gave it me at the Gate House.'

'Who?' asked Man, not touching it.

'The ironmonger, of course.'

'Whose is it, then?'

The waiter passed behind the watchman with another load of dishes.

'Well, 'twas his at first, then mine, then Mr Trippuck's. A – gift of sorts. He says as he found it this morn at Zachary's house, and then he throws it into my face.'

'For what reason?'

'Of that I know nothing, Sir,' the widow said quickly. 'But he was in a shaking rage over it and left the room with a black face to search out Mr Trippuck himself. I do not fear for Zachary as he stands: he's too much man for the ironmonger. But Robin does his best work from the back and in the dark.' She stood up and smoothed her dress. 'If you still mean to follow this business to its end, Sir, I would have you sound the streets for Alan Fletcher. I can see you do not yet know him enough.'

After Judith Woodman had left the tavern, the watchman sat on through three pipefuls, staring dumbly before him into the clinging smoke that dimmed the room. The interview had not gone as he had wanted and expected, but he felt somehow that he knew more now than if it had.

He knew where he had made his mistake. He had let the mere circumstances of the widow's actions – and his own more complex feelings towards her – blind him to the simple realities of her character. It no longer mattered where she was last night or even that she could not have been where she claimed. Now Man fully believed that what she had initially told him was the truth – that she had been in her room above the ironmonger's shop all evening – and that she had later lied to Constable Burton out of fear and caution. But the bare fact that she could have murdered Joan Fletcher now meant nothing.

Because Judith Woodman was a shrewd and prudent, practical and manipulating woman who would have little interest in doing anything that could not bring her money and the power that always comes with it. Man now suspected that for the past three years the widow had been steadily extorting money and gifts from the ironmonger in return for her silence. If that were the case, it would help to explain much: the ironmonger's continuing need for more money, his deep resentment of the widow, her own stopping so long at the shop. It must have been an agonizing situation for Alan Fletcher – the three of them alone together – but a most satisfying one for Judith Woodman, one which it could never profit her to change.

The watchman pocketed the anodyne necklace and tried to stop the waiter for his bill. Man felt troubled, worried. He sensed that the pace of events had been stepped up, that everything connected with the killing was beginning to move too fast for him. Alan Fletcher was gone, no one knew to where. He was angry, the kind of mindless flaming anger only the meek can know. If he now knew of the relationship between the widow and Zachary Trippuck, what might he be thinking? And if he imagined that the two of them had been working together against him, what might he be planning?

Man made his way slowly towards the stairwell of the cellar-tavern. The room held perhaps two or three dozen people, each one of whom was talking or laughing or resting. Some were fighting: a few, weeping. Each of them had a unique and convoluted history, compounded of memories and needs and fears that no one else could ever wholly know. The multiplicity of it all overwhelmed the young watchman – and also somehow elated him.

Outside, Man was surprised to find the wind shifted about to the north and gusting heavily again. The debris that had been tumbled up the streets the night before now seemed determined to be returned to their rightful places. The people stumbled, looking up at the great sombre cloud that was advancing upon the city. Man smelled the new slick fragrance of hidden rain. He crammed his hat more firmly upon his head and set off, his thoughts on the ironmonger and the widow and on the waiter's neat stacks of dishes.

Madam Betty Gierih was standing ankle-deep in rubble and just below the yawning hole in the ceiling, doing her best to bother the workmen with superfluous advice and not forgetting to stand on their hammers whenever they needed them. She wore a grey tent of a nightgown, and her man's voice was clear: it was a part of her policy never to dress or drink during the hours of daylight. She seemed not to feel the keenness of the wind sweeping through the remnants of the roof nor to notice the dark cloud that was filling in the hole.

'Let the draperies clear the dust, for the love of God!' Two workmen hoisted the bed-frame higher. 'Nay, lad, you may have cast dust in the lights of them in this room, but Madam Betty's not to be hoodwinked so nicely. I guessed you on the watch as soon as you walked in. I read it in your feet.'

She bustled about, the nightgown showing more than it hid. The workmen leered over their shoulders and snickered at each other.

'But why should you think, lad, that poor Robin Fletcher would be cooling his hoofs at the Cock and Bull? 'Tis his second home, that's true enough; but with the sadness that's on him now?' She turned with a snarl. 'Mind what you're at with that chair, Sirrah, there's a piece of it'll stand still.' She laid a hand upon her bosom and sighed. 'And me just hearing of it at first light. Dear, dear Joany Parker! Ugly, ain't it? Why, I can almost see her in this very room again, doing her night's duty, and it's been ten year or more.'

Madam Betty wiped a tear from one eye, while the other was trained critically upon the clumsiest of the workmen.

'Worked here? Of course she worked here. As have many of the finest mistresses in Westminster. Four, five year or more she stayed on here. Came to me out of hunger at the first, as the most of them do, and then held on for comfort. She favoured the trade, too, until Robin stepped in with the fairer offer.'

She was gone suddenly in a flurry of nightgown and leg to inspect the clearing away of the wreckage. Some bricks and tiles might be salvageable, if the workmen would only take care. She returned in a minute, mumbling figures.

'Can you credit that, lad? These hobberdehoys are for telling me that this night's wind has uplifted the cost of the pantiles from fifty shillings to ten pounds to the thousand. And six for the plain! And the bricklayers are promising to ask five shillings for a mere day. I'll have to fall back upon deal boards at this!' She gnawed at the scrawny hairs above her lip. 'And fool Robin chooses this time of all to be in with a works that lies idle and unmanned. If you look for him, boy, I would send you to where he ought to be: at Tilbury Town, pressing the bricks and trimming the tiles with his own soft hands!'

The wind was now filling the room, picking away at the edges of the hole in the ceiling and stirring up the mounds of brick-dust into the workmen's eyes. A few drops of rain began to darken the floor. A lengthening roll of thunder made the woman jerk.

'God's ballocks, if we're not facing another night of it! And me with no more'n the half of a roof over me.' She yelled a few incoherent orders at the workmen and turned back. 'Aye, he's an ill-fated one is the ironmonger. And after Madam Betty's done all that she's able for him. Why, wasn't it this July last that I handed him a pretty purse of cash to help him see a way through his troubles? And have I yet seen the shadow of any of it coming back to me? Yet a bit before, at the tail-end of May it was, comes the man to this house with fifty of the cleanest guineas that ever opened your eye. And what's he want me to do with it? Why, take it to pay on some house or other for him outside the town! What? For Joany herself?' She twisted her mouth and made a rude noise. 'And do I ever taste the least skimming off it myself for my bother? Pah! Get a fart off a dead man as soon as a farthing off him!'

A circle of the girls had come to the door of the room to stare and giggle at the workmen. Susan was among them. She looked shyly towards the other end of the room.

Madam Betty was off again, this time fussing noisily on behalf of the paper-hangings. On her third circuit about the walls, she stopped to resume the conversation.

'Where'd he come by the guineas, then? No idea, lad. Yet he handled them as daintily as though they were St Judas's own. And now they're in the house that's promised him – I won't say where. And knowing well enough what this same room saw a twelvemonth agone, I can tell you he won't be left to enjoy the place in his lonesomeness.' She closed one shrivelled eyelid expressively. 'Not even now.'

A sudden outbreak of thunder brought a chilling spray of rain through the roof. The girls fled shrieking downstairs, and the men lounged smiling against the walls. Madam Betty stood planted to the floor, hands on hips and elbows jutted out, cursing the elements.

The wind and rain finally cooled her, and she became more serious and pensive.

'Yet I question whether you've quite understood it aright.

What passed between Joany Parker and Robin is nor so simple or uncommon as you might think. Ask Madam Betty, lad: she's stroked the underside of it often enough to know.' She came a step closer. 'Now God made man and he made woman, and he made them – as even a greenhead as you should know – he fashioned them to fit together. Now some say that the fitting together is ne'er anything but smooth and troubleless – that's what my girls here will tell you. But there's a rub lies here, and it's naught so small as a forgetful rub-belly in the dark neither!' The woman raised her voice above the noise of the workmen's talking and the entering wind. 'You've asked me, lad, the history of the ironmonger's in Green's Alley, and I'll tell you the whole of it in Homer's own nutshell. Robin could not rest himself well with the knowing he's ne'er been first in and first out with any one dame – not even his own. Nothing could run more simpler than that now, could it? And that kind of lay always works a deep wrongness in a man that can't be eased till he has cleared the debt – one way or the other.'

The shower had moved off now, the workmen had bent to their tools again. Madam Betty had nothing more to say.

When most of the wreckage had been shovelled away, the indecent blow-book was found under the crushed table where it had been forgotten the night before. It was opened to a childishly drawn sketch of a very young girl lying naked and hurt in the midst of a dark spreading stain.

When, in 1699, Ned Ward moved his punch-shop and tavern from Moorfields to Fulwood's Rents just off Holbourn Court, Gray's Inn, his old customers followed him faithfully and even brought him in new ones. It could have been Ned's special milk-punch that kept them stopping in, the secret recipe for which he had himself brought back from the West Indies: two quarts old milk, one quart long-kept rum, six lemons, six ounces loaf sugar, one nutmeg finely grated – served in a broad bowl with freshly toasted biscuits floating on top. It was a drink that could flavour talk of religion or politics or the war equally well: Ned had even been able to persuade some of his stoutest Tory friends to prefer it to their beloved Malaga sack.

Yet the success of his shop could just as well have been due to Ned himself. Everybody wanted to trade tales with the notorious 'London Spy' whose humorous exploits had just been reprinted 'compleat, in eighteen parts', in octavo. All agreed that Ned knew as much as could be known about any of the more important poets and authors of the town and that he would talk of what should not be told even more readily than of what should. There was not a tavern or coffee-house he had not visited, nor a lady from whom he had not contracted some disease. He could talk any man's language – the sailor's, the higgler's, the coney-catcher's – and answer them phrase for phrase. If all else failed, he would merrily describe his project for doing 'The Life and Notable Adventures of Don Quixote de la Mancha' into Hudibrastic verse.

The truth was: Ned Ward knew men. Ask anyone who knew him – everyone did – and they would tell you the same thing: Ned Ward could take the right measure of any man just by looking at him. And right now, as he stood surveying his half-filled shop, he was thinking that he did not at all like the look on that cove sitting over there, that one keeping himself to himself in the outside corner.

He had come in with the cloud, so to say. Just when the wind had begun to pick up again, this time from the north, bringing before it the face of a long piece of cloud that was blackening the city street by street and turning the talk to the worry of a return of last night's storm. He had sidled in, looking as discomforted as an Aminadab in a stew, and lowered himself on to his pin-buttock in the darkest and loneliest part of the shop. The bowl of punch that had been set before him had been left untasted; he did not smoke. He was timid and insignificant, seemingly reduced in size; and the look of his skin in shadow reminded Ned Ward that he had a load of lemon pulp to dispose of. A blubbering flogging-cully, thought Ned, by the woebegone face on him.

The thing was, Ned knew him. Not by name, but he had seen him time and again in some stinking hummum or other. In Madam Betty's Cock and Bull probably – that would fit him as a pudding fits a friar's mouth. A muddy bird of a man, setting himself to take the great leap in the dark into some poor girl's unwarded pump-dale. In a moment Ned had the name: Robin.

What worried Ned Ward most about the man was neither his sickened appearance nor his maddening fidgeting about in his chair, but the intense yet furtive way he kept staring at one particular section of the room. He was looking at a boxed-in table where two men were sitting, drinking heavily and talking loudly. And Ned was all but sure that the one in the outside corner was a fast friend to the pair at the table: he had seen them in company before, sporting together in the greatest boisterousness.

Now to Ned Ward's way of thinking, a man simply does not walk into a punch-shop and tavern where his mates are busy enjoying themselves without coming over at once to join them or at least hailing them from across the room. This was what bothered him so – the unnaturalness of it – the way the man called Robin hid himself from his friends. As for the two at the table, they had not seen the other enter. Ned knew them, too. Young Jack Smith held his dislocated arm gingerly before him on the table; he looked near to fainting, his face greenish and blurred by pain. Zachary Trippuck – loud, swaggering, coarse – was the same as ever.

Ned Ward looked again across the room at the man in the outside corner. He was still gazing fixedly at his friends, now with a yearning expression as if he wanted to draw them closer to him. A man might die happy, Ned said to himself, with just such a look as that from a lechery-layer in bunting time. Or from his own good wife, once in a blue moon.

Through the punch-shop's two small windows, Ned saw the wind tumbling the passers-by into a series of ridiculous gesticulations. There was the unreal light of an eclipse in the air.

Ned had to help his man see to the needs of the customers; but as he circulated among the tables and the odd chairs, he could not help glancing over his shoulder time and again at the man alone in the corner. Something was going to happen, he could feel it; something great and inevitable.

'Mr Ward! Sirrah!'

'Yours, Mr Trippuck.'

The man's mouth slackened with drunkenness. 'Have you no fare more worthy of a man's tongue than this womanish swill?'

Ned Ward did not much care for the man's tone. He very slowly stripped a sliver of wood from a low ceiling beam, rammed it between two front teeth, and dislodged a bit of this morning's orange. It vaulted to the centre of the table.

'Two cups of the cowslip mead, then?' he said affably, naming the drink ladies preferred during their morning visits.

Zachary Trippuck's face reddened horribly. He turned towards his friend with a scowl, but Jack Smith was weaving in his chair like an enthusiast from Bedlam. Ned Ward felt an

172

urge to offer the young man a tin plate to tie upon his injured arm – the traditional badge of the licensed mad beggar – then thought better of it.

There was a long moment during which Zachary Trippuck's left hand strayed negligently across his stomach towards the short sword hanging at his hip and Ned Ward's feet squared and his knees bent slightly. Both men were ready, but Ned had lived through too many such scenes to feel or show any fear. Then the moment passed.

'The cowslip for yourself, Sir!' Trippuck shouted with a brittle laugh. 'Roll-me-in-the-kennel for us! Geneva, man, the worst you have!'

After this, Ned Ward tried to keep himself as close to the boxed-in table as he dared without arousing Trippuck's intoxicated anger. If anything rough was in the offing, he meant to be a part of it – to stop it or to finish it. This was his shop.

Once he ventured over to wait upon the nervous man in the outside corner.

'If the milk-punch be not to your favour, Sir, I can quickly mix you a fine shrub or a sweet Sir Cloudesley that would bring Mr Shovell himself in from his present troubles at the Gunfleet.' Ned had eyed the full bowl with a look that would have shamed any other customer to his stockings.

'No – really, Sir – no! This suits me well enough, I assure you.' The man picked listlessly at the soggy, disintegrating biscuits. 'I take my drink very slowly as a habit.'

'You can please yourself best, Sir.' As Ned turned away, he saw the man called Robin resume his uneasy staring at his two friends across the room. This time, he was surprised to find in the man's white face the tense creases of jealousy and a cold mean hatred.

'Damned trugmoldy's bastard!' Ned Ward muttered bitterly

to himself as he walked away. 'Tell him to carry his foul spitefulness out of my house!'

Zachary Trippuck was talking more loudly now, loudly enough for the whole shop to hear. His thick voice mimicked the beginnings of the thunder overhead.

'A hard death indeed for the woman, as you say, Jack m'lad, a hard death. But something harder, I fear me, for myself at the long run. Here sees an end, then, to the careful plucking of one Tom Cony.'

Jack Smith said something, but Ned was not close enough to hear.

'Nor did any man else. I'm a close-fitted man with my secrets, Jack, and so is the lady. And as for that cully himself, 'twas always our thought that he's a man as well-hung in his hidden pockets as he is light-hung in his breeches.'

Trippuck's raw laughter drowned out Jack Smith's words.

'Nay, the game might be played at yet. Are you forgetting Alex Woodman, m'lad? And who was it, then, that led us all into that?'

The rain came with a suddenness that surprised everyone, a heavy squall of wind-blown water that rattled against the walls and pockmarked the dry surface of the road. Most of the men in the punch-shop divided themselves between the two front windows to see. Ned Ward went over, too, and in a moment he felt the lurching body of Zachary Trippuck pressing into him from behind.

The men watched the rain and talked of the storm – of the loss of life at sea and on the river, of the loss or spoiling of merchandise. The storm had made of the city a single being, and the damage done to one was felt by all.

Then Ned Ward heard from directly behind him a quick succession of three distinctive sounds.

The first was a tiny slippery sound which he recognized at once – the high-pitched sighing of a sword being pulled from its leather scabbard. Then a low puffing noise, a fork driven into overripe fruit. And last a deep hollow grunt as of a man trying to lift an impossibly heavy weight.

He turned into the face of Zachary Trippuck. The man looked stricken and doubtful, as if he were trying to understand the meaning of a new and untranslatable word. Ned Ward looked down and saw that Trippuck's coat was pointing outward, as though he had suddenly grown one breast. Then the man collapsed against him, and somebody pushed his way through the crowd and out the door.

Ned glanced through the dead man's tousled hair. The man in the outside corner was gone.

After leaving the Cock and Bull bagnio, George Man felt an even stronger need to continue his search for Alan Fletcher. The ironmonger now appeared to him as a driven and unstable man, capable of anything. Man was certain he would find Fletcher and Zachary Trippuck together, and it made him afraid.

Some of Madam Betty's girls had mentioned that the men often roamed the Park in the early evenings, before moving on to the taverns and brothels. The watchman could check Duck Island first before nightfall, and then he could question whichever people happened to be at the Royal Cockpit. Although he was reluctant to admit it to himself, he was eager for an excuse for stopping in at Dartmouth Street again. He wanted to see Sarah Wells.

But he never made it. He was half way across King Street – savouring the rain-freshened air and the gentler wind – when he heard someone crying out for a watchman in a high, warbling voice.

Running up the street in a comical flapping gallop came the Reverend William Derham. His cheeks were glowing, and his mouth was spread in a demoniacal grin of exertion. Man politely moved a few steps forward to meet him.

'Well met, Sir.'

The vicar laid a hand upon the young watchman's shoulder to steady himself as he tried to catch his breath.

'Well, it is a happy chance our coming together in the street like this, is it not? And everyone in Upminster talks of London as being such a monstrous large and lonely place. Why, one meets a friend at almost any turning!'

Derham oscillated slightly from side to side, and Man decided there was probably a bit more drink than exercise in the Reverend's burning face.

'You have come from Hell then, have you, Sir?'

'What's that? From where?' It took him a confused moment to remember. 'Oh! That tavern you spoke of earlier. Well, no – I mean to say, the gentlemen were obliged to end the gathering early. This last night has left many of their affairs in a sad disarray, sad. But we did manage to please ourselves quite well enough at that house called Purgatory. Or – wait a bit – was it the Heaven we were last at?'

The two stood still in the moving traffic of King Street, Man looking at the muddled Reverend with quiet affection.

'But what was it, then,' asked Derham after a moment, 'that you wished to talk with me about, Sir?'

'I, Sir?' Man said, embarrassed. 'Nothing, I think.'

'What? But I thought . . . Yet that could have been another.' Derham tried to twitch up his glasses and missed. They hung at a precarious angle across his face. 'But you have, as I remember, expressed some especial interest in Mr Fletcher and in his – his present situation. You might, in that case, now want to accompany me on a visit of an hour or two.'

'To Mr Defoe?'

'Why, yes, the same. It was a gentleman whom I have just left told me that he knew somewhat of Alan Fletcher and Mr Defoe together – that is to say, that he knew they followed some business or other together and that the ironmonger, in his current difficulties, might well turn to Defoe first for relief. It was his thought that they might be even now laying their heads together in conversation.'

''Tis possible,' the watchman mused, 'if only that.'

The Reverend brightened up considerably. 'Well, I should be most happy of your society this afternoon, Sir. The truth is –' he hesitated and squinted uncertainly up the road – 'God's own truth is, I am not completely satisfied of knowing my way. Is Spitalfields far, do you know?'

Imperceptibly, with neither man noticing, the two had begun to drift together up King Street.

Man was feeling a concern and a friendliness towards the good vicar that surprised and comforted him. With Derham, he did not feel quite so young and inexperienced. Suddenly, the problem of finding the ironmonger and the mystery of the death of Joan Fletcher seemed somehow less immediate, less pressing. There was a chance, too, that he might be able to learn something of importance from the man, Defoe.

'Have you ever met the fellow, then?' Derham asked, now walking much more steadily.

'Mr Defoe? No, not formally.' Man smiled at some private amusement.

'A virtuous man, I think, though somewhat given to a certain errantness in his actions. He is, as you must know, a thorough-paced Dissenter; but I have never let that hinder me from regarding him as a brother under God and as a sincere and valuable friend.'

The two men walked on in stride, their shoulders occasionally bumping together. The wind was brisk and clean, but it had lost its wildness.

'If he has a fault,' Man said carefully, 'I should say it is that he plies his pen a mite too promiscuously and without due consideration. Everyone agrees, I think, that the pamphlet was mistimed.'

'Miscreated, rather,' said Derham, shaking his head with a long sigh. 'To add fuel to the people's already flaming passions is bad enough: Dr Henry Sacheverell himself incautiously did as much at Oxford in June of last year. But for Mr Defoe to have confused the mob with a mere ruse and that at his own party's expense . . . Well!'

The watchman and the Reverend kept silence between them for most of their walk, each of them busy with his own thoughts. The city continued working at the shambles left by the storm: men could be seen wheeling loads of new bricks and tiles into broken houses from which low, tired sobbing could often be heard. The people still looked up suspiciously at the darkening sky, but now their talk sounded more relieved than panicked. And many seemed simply astonished to have survived.

However weighty and theological the thoughts of the Reverend William Derham may have been, those of George Man were undoubtedly more practical and in fuller detail. He had lived through the controversies and tensions that had run through the streets of the city during the last decade, and he himself had even become indirectly involved in the curious part played by the one-time Cornhill hosier, Daniel Defoe.

To Man, the long-standing antagonism between the Church of England and its supporters and the various groups of Dissenters had never seemed especially difficult to understand. There was the basic issue of conscience, of course: the

Nonconformists simply demanded the right to worship as they chose, while their opponents defended the solidarity of the Church and of the state. Yet as Man saw it, there were not finally such very great differences between the two – not so much, at least, to account for the bitterness and the savagery of the conflict.

For Man's view of the scene was from the level of the street, and his experience of it came from his talking and listening to the crowd. He knew it was the fact that most of the Dissenters were Whigs of the trading class that weighed most heavily with the common man of the city. When the mercenary spirit and the mean social level of the merchant were combined with the irksome fervour of the religious independent, it was no wonder that both the Tory gentleman and the High Church zealot – not to mention the harried chairman and the unlettered hawker – felt suspicious and unkindly towards the eccentric Dissenter. And no one could quite forget that it had been the Dissenter's father or grandfather who had helped to kill an English king: many still sang street-ballads of the beheading of Charles I fifty-four years ago.

Man and Derham had by now passed through the Strand, once more thronged with impatient shoppers, and entered Fleet Street without exchanging more than a few words between them. The watchman, following the line of his thoughts, suddenly remembered that his father had once employed as foreman at the brewery a man who had lived in some side-alley near here. A Dissenter – a joyless, meditative, fault-finding sort of fellow whom neither Man nor his father had ever much liked. There had never been anything greatly wrong with the man, only the nagging way his overgrown seriousness had kept constantly calling attention to itself. He took his religion with his breakfast, and it gave a bitter taste to your morning draught. He would never write even a letter on a Sunday, and his repeating it made you suddenly wish you hadn't. He was emotional and furtive: he would retire into prayer in the same way the drunkard hides himself with a bottle.

Under William, as Man recalled, the Dissenters had enjoyed a period of relative tranquillity. But as soon as Anne had come to the throne last year, things had begun to worsen. The Queen was a self-conscious champion of the state church: some suggested that she was far more interested in the Church than in God. Her unguarded statements had given rise to such fiery outbursts of High Church fanaticism as that mentioned by William Derham. 'Down with the Whigs' had been shouted in the streets; harmless ministers were insulted, even beaten. Then in November the House of Commons had passed by a comfortable majority a harsh bill against Occasional Conformity – that curious practice whereby a Dissenter could hold public office by means of an occasional sham communion in the established church. The bill had failed in the House of Lords, but the mood that had inspired it had not. Finally, in December of 1702, a highly inflammatory pamphlet had appeared on the streets: *The Shortest Way with the Dissenters.*

Man had read it: who had not? The text had all the irrational indignation of a High Church diatribe against the Dissenters, advocating a quick return to the glorious days of fire and faggot. All half-measures were to be stopped; the vermin infesting the country must be eradicated at once. The coffee-houses of the city had hummed with talk of it. Man had seen the pamphlet being passed from hand to hand – either above or beneath the table, depending upon the persuasion prevailing at the house. When the anonymous author was discovered to be Daniel Defoe – himself the staunchest of Dissenters – the city-wide excitement had changed to stunned confusion. No one could have suspected such a reckless and ingenious jest. It was only later that Man had begun to see the irony in the writing, the deliberate exaggeration of the fanatic's stand that was meant to draw out and expose to ridicule the Church's approved intolerance. But nobody had appreciated the trick, least of all the Dissenters themselves. It had seemed to all much like a man's giving cannons to two angry duellists and then standing well back, ready to laugh.

The watchman's thoughts were interrupted by the Reverend's worrying that they had lost their way. They had already passed through St Paul's Churchyard and most of Cheapside and were now coming into Cornhill. Derham's directions were vague enough: he knew only that Defoe was staying a few days at a friend's house – a French weaver living somewhere in Spitalfields, but the vicar simply could not recall the man's name. The watchman was hoping that Defoe's recent notoriety in the streets would help lead them to him.

It was as the two passed by on the south side of the Royal Exchange that Man remembered Daniel Defoe's first stand in the pillory. It had been near here, a Thursday, the twenty-ninth day of July. Man had been one of those assigned to keep order, but it had turned out not to be necessary. Instead of throwing insults and garbage, the spectators had cheered and thrown garlands of fresh flowers.

The Crown's justice had been swift and severe. The Earl of Nottingham – 'Dismal' to his enemies – had issued a warrant for Defoe's arrest on 3 January 1703, and the fugitive had finally been taken on the advice of an informer towards the end of May. The trial had come as a surprise to no one: the quick-tongued Simon Harcourt had argued wonderfully for the Queen, and Defoe's lawyer, William Colepeper, had made the bad mistake of advising his friend to plead guilty. But the sentence was a shock: three times in the pillory, a fine of two hundred marks, imprisonment, and sureties for his conduct during the next seven years. Man had known plenty of violent thieves and bullies who had received far milder sentences or none at all.

And by the end of July, the mood of the people had swung almost completely to the other side. What had the poor fellow done, after all, that was so terribly wrong? Only spoke his mind, and maybe showed up the High Church meanness for what it really was. If that was to be called seditious libel and the man must lie in gaol for it, then there were enough others that should lie there with him for company. Defoe in the pillory had become the good citizen who was being unjustly punished for personal reasons outside of the law. It had been an odd sort of triumph for him, bent painfully over and smiling. The hawkers had run the street with the author's newest work: *Hymn to the Pillory*, an audacious satire. Man had bought a copy of it himself, without anyone's noticing.

Now, as the watchman and Derham neared Spitalfields, Man found himself growing more and more excited. If Alan Fletcher did have business dealings with Defoe, then both they and the ironmonger must have suffered during the man's lying in Newgate. And Defoe had just now come out. Suddenly, the idea of finding Alan Fletcher somewhere near or even with Daniel Defoe did not seem as absurd to the watchman as it had before.

Man hurried the Reverend on into the falling dusk. They moved by or through groups of men and groups of boys who were talking and wondering about the pale man who had just run past, heading towards Spitalfields. He was flying as if he felt the Devil himself in his tail.

Chapter 4

As the sad and remarkable disasters of this terrible night
were full of a dismal variety, so the goodness of
Providence, in the many remarkable deliverances both
by sea and land, have their share in this account, as they
claim an equal variety and wonder.

'No, Sir, I cannot swear to know Mr Fletcher at all deeply. The
contriving of business together has been our only contact at all
times. And in any instance the sociate is as far from the friend
as the friend is from the brother.'

Daniel Defoe sat across from George Man, and the two talked
as easily as if they had known each other for years. The
watchman had at first felt shy and clumsy in the company of
the infamous pamphleteer, but Defoe had a talent for talking
informally with any class of stranger. He could charm a fishwife,
Man imagined, as well as persuade a lord.

The watchman and Defoe sat near the meagre fire in the upstairs room, while the Reverend William Derham and their host,
Nathaniel Sammen – a tall, incredibly sedate man – stood debating
religion in a cold corner. The storm had already been discussed
by all; the second glass of ale had just been poured. Man's pipe
was scorching his hand, and Defoe was leaning forward eagerly,
obviously relishing what he enjoyed most – conversation.

Man could notice little change in Defoe since he had seen him last in July. The high and broad forehead was still unlined, and the sloping nose still reminded him of the prow of a running ship. His own hair hung long and only half-combed. The eyes were large and as intent as before, only now they looked out of a deep weariness instead of fear and anger. Too much had happened to Defoe this year.

'Might I ask you, Sir, how it was that you came first to meet the man?' The watchman asked his questions with a certain hesitation, still somewhat in awe of Defoe's recent history.

'It was in, I think, 'ninety-six that I was myself much in Westminster to watch over some few dealings that I had in view there. Every man, you know, has sometime the thought to stir his finger in the mortar till it sticks. I meant to bring down two of the old timber houses that lay next to the Woolstaple Market and build in their stead twelve brick houses which would have opened a clear way from the market to the river. The projection came to nothing, but I did meet Mr Fletcher through the agency of another man whose name I have now forgot – a loud man with a lameness in his leg. As it fell out, Mr Fletcher and myself came to some talk of Tilbury and my then-new brickworks there. He showed enough concern to pay a way for himself into it. He was most ready, as I remember it, to find himself in something that lay somewhere outside the town, and my works seemed to like him full enough.'

'Did he run ever to view the place with you?' Man was thinking of the letter that the boy from the tavern in Green's Alley had taken yesterday to the ironmonger's shop.

Defoe's face drew itself together with all the appearance of a shopkeeper figuring a total. 'There was – yes – the first occasion was in the winter of that same year. November, if not after. I recall it for the hard and frozen journey we had of it in the flying-coach. Snow, too, Sir, if you can mind it. One of the decade's deepest winters in selected parts of the country. Mr Derham here can quote you the inches of it, I've little doubt.'

The watchman almost smiled. Daniel Defoe had the merchant's love of exactness, the real affection for enumeration that Man's own father had always shown and which his son had never been able to appreciate.

Man set his pipe aside and took up his ale. He looked down steadily into his glass, and his voice cracked with embarrassment.

'Did Mr Fletcher chance, at any of his visits to Tilbury, to meet any one woman or girl with whom he could have enjoyed a private conversation? The question is indelicate, Sir,' Man hurried to add, 'but my reasons for asking it are grave.'

Defoe took some time to answer. He had at first looked shocked at the question; then he noticed the watchman's seriousness and began to pull studiously at the sharp end of his nose.

'As to that, Sir, I think I neither can nor should say much. We did stop always at the house of my clerk and superintendent, Mr Castleton. He's a daughter – a pretty enough girl and rightly quiet – who did walk out to the works with the men the odd time. I saw no sin in it myself, Sir. The girl – Pamela, her name is – was but an untried maid of ten or eleven when the man made his first visit to Tilbury. Now, of course, she's a woman grown; and as to her father, I can answer for him myself. He's a hard-handed man with the brickmakers and with his own family and has the ill-polished manners of the carman, but he's a fair man withal and exemplary in almost everything he does.'

Defoe paused and suddenly looked at the watchman almost accusingly. 'If you know something, Sir, against either Fletcher or the girl, you would do well to know it fully before speaking. I myself know nothing of what has or has not passed between them; but the girl is old enough to choose her own way with her father's word, and the man is not too old for it and never married. He may be somewhat fey on the face of him, but I think he sees a goldsmith's note from a gelding when it comes to his pockets – and that's enough to say of any man!' The pamphleteer sat back with a satisfied grunt.

Neither the watchman nor Derham had yet made any mention of the death of Joan Fletcher; and now Man sat slowly nodding his head, as if he had just heard what he had been expecting to hear.

The room was growing darker and colder, and the Reverend and Nathaniel Sammen had retired to a small table with a candle. The weaver's wife came into the room with a pitcher of fresh ale, and she quickly filled all the men's glasses in turn – all the while smoothly pretending that she was not there.

'And the girl,' Man went on, thoughtfully cleaning the corners of his mouth, 'this Pamela Castleton. Do you know, Sir, if she ever came herself up here to the city?'

'Why, she did at that. Once. That is to say, she ran up with her father and a few others. A year ago this month – no, look you, Sir – a year ago this very week it was. That's a far chance now, is it not? We men had much to talk on for the business: some fool-headed buyer was favouring the pink and half-done Sammel bricks over our own. They please the eye, Sir, I admit it at once; but they have no quality, no texture, no true tone when struck. They cannot hold with time.'

'And did Mr Fletcher make one of your company at that juncture?'

Defoe took a moment to think. 'No, I do not remember that he was with us. What, Sir, should it signify if he was?'

Man adroitly avoided the question. 'Yet the girl herself was not with you always.'

'No, no. She carried a servant-maid about with her to shop the city. She was, as I understand it, upon her first visit: and she wanted, as the ladies will, to study the labelled prices in the shops.'

'*And knowing well enough what this same room saw a twelvemonth agone, I can tell you he won't be left to enjoy the place in his lonesomeness.*' Madam Betty Gierih knew her own business very well indeed: they would need a place for it.

'I suppose, Sir,' Man said delicately, 'that the business has not been doing so well of late.'

'That is so. My – absence from the scene has unhappily allowed too many orders to miss the mark.' Defoe seemed for a moment to become angry – Man could see his narrow shoulders hunch – but then he got control of himself again. 'My own people are not without blame in this matter, Sir. You must know that since the Toleration Act of sixteen-eighty-nine many of our meeting-houses have been covered in the pantiles as a distinguishing mark. Now when my hand in the pamphlet was made known and my course towards Newgate was set, most of the orders from the Dissenters fell off or were withdrawn. It pained me much, Sir, and pushed the business off its legs, but I do not know that I can fault them just there. They follow what is right: and if they sometimes must bend the knee to convenience, it counts but little so long as they return to the right at the end.'

The watchman edged his chair an inch closer to Defoe's and settled his hands in his lap. He was beginning to feel more comfortable now with the merchant-pamphleteer and with Defoe's easy merging of shrewd common sense and active moral ideals.

'I should think this girl – this Pamela Castleton – is yet at her father's house in Tilbury?'

'I could not say, Sir. But the Gravesend tiltboats ferry fifty at a time to and from London. You might go yourself to see, if you think it needful.'

'Are there no coaches for tomorrow, then?' Man had always feared travel by water. 'I am to work within the hour.'

'Raymond Chambers drives as good a team as any, and he does his best trade on the Sunday.' A nagging petulance came into his voice. 'It is my thought, Sir, that the suffering the coachmen to ply for hire on the Sabbath was the single black mark upon the otherwise noble reign of the late King – a man who honoured me, Sir, with his especial love.'

It was all Man could do to steer the conversation gradually towards an end. He took out his watch a dozen times, each time with a more worried shake of the head; he cleaned his pipe with a straw until the straw broke; he half-rose from his chair again and again, his legs shaking with the strain. It was only when Derham and the weaver finally stepped across the room to join in the talk that Man felt himself free to go.

He put one last question to Defoe.

'Have you, Sir, happened to see Alan Fletcher at all recently?' After he had said it, Man wished he had not: whom could a man in gaol see?

'The last was a week I shall not soon forget, Sir, the third in May. He was come to this very house to speak with me of the bricks, but I was not to be seen. A few days after, I was taken here by the Queen's officers, the mean work of some foul spy who valued the fifty-guinea reward over his own soul's honour.'

Defoe still spoke of the ironmonger as a trusted business partner, but Man could remember only the sum of money which Fletcher had handed over to Betty Gierih to invest for him in a new house. Fifty pounds. In May.

The watchman said nothing and left the house. It was too

late now to help or hurt Daniel Defoe: his worst troubles were behind him. And Man suspected that it was now too late for Alan Fletcher as well.

Man did not know the Spitalfields area at all well: most of the streets and the shops were new to him, and hearing at least half of the people he passed speaking French or imperfect English made him feel as though he were entering another world. But Defoe's directions had been explicit enough, and Man soon found himself standing before the Lame Horse Coaching Inn.

He could not say why he had come here. Defoe had assured him that there were no night-coaches on Saturdays, and Man needed to hurry back to Westminster as soon as possible. He would come late to his work as it was. During his walk over, he had promised himself repeatedly that he would only stop in for a moment to make certain that there was a flying-coach to Tilbury on Sunday and to secure himself a place in it if he could. And all the time he knew that he could do this just as well tomorrow morning.

So much had happened in the last twenty-four hours, Man had become involved in so many people's lives – and in one woman's death – that he no longer felt able to see things clearly or to think about what he did or did not know. Now he knew only that the coaching-inn and Tilbury were the next places he must go. If he could not yet understand everything completely, he could still move, still watch.

The Lame Horse Coaching Inn was no different from any other of its kind. It had a dry drive thirty yards long, an arched entry into a rectangular courtyard, four coach-houses, stabling for twenty-five horses, thirty bedrooms, and more coffee-rooms and dining-parlours than it needed. The proprietor was a Jew, transplanted from Muscovy: his wife was rumoured to be a witch. The inn was usually crowded with trade: most of the coaches for Chelmsford and Colchester, and a few for Cambridge, left from here and put in here on their return.

The storm had changed everything. Man saw only three or four coaches in the darkening courtyard, only one with a driver. The few people moving about seemed all to belong to the inn. The watchman walked over to the coach with the driver and stood in the small circle shed by the courtyard's only light.

The flying-coach looked as if it had just come in from a long and rough journey: mud caked the sides to the windows, one wheel stood at a dangerous slant, and the horses were still sweating and wheezing. The driver seemed even more worn than the horses. He sat slumped over with the reins and whip in his hands, the brim of his stained hat cracked down over his face. He could have been asleep, but for the steady motion of his jaw, as if he were thinking as laboriously as a cow at grass. Man had to speak loudly twice to rouse him.

'For Tilbury on the morrow. You've it right that far, Sir.'

'You would appear, friend, to have driven through the teeth of last night's storm.'

'Last night, this morn, 'n' this afternoon. We breaked down on the wild road, too. Wouldn't be here now, if not for a farmer and a ox.'

'From Tilbury itself, then?'

The driver looked at Man with the natural suspicion of the country for the city. 'Where else, then?'

The watchman leaned casually against the side of the coach. He could feel the shivering of the horses through the wood.

'Much fare?'

Raymond Chambers made a sound that could have been a tired grunt or the number 'one'.

'I will tell you, friend,' Man said slowly, not looking towards the driver, 'that Miss Pamela Castleton is expected here tonight, and we make ourselves most anxious for her welcoming.' A bluff, of course: but whom else from Tilbury did Man know by name?

This time the driver expressed himself even more succinctly. A spreading ball of spit sailed lazily over the side of the coach and fell through the dark air to coat the toe of the watchman's boot. Man smiled to himself at the accuracy of the gesture.

'I mean to help her, friend.' He moved over to pat the twitching rump of one of the horses. 'I think to know more of this affair than you, Sir. Or the young lady herself. I promise you she is running towards great harm.'

This started the driver upon a long bout of thinking. Over the background murmur of the courtyard and the distant street, Man could hear the thick grinding of teeth.

'A man might tell another man a flick more about it.'

'When I know more, yes. But the helping the girl step clear of it is first.'

The watchman's concern for Pamela Castleton decided it. Raymond Chambers pointed with his whip towards a pair of lighted windows.

'She's in the coffee-room with 'im. She bid me to my own bed, but I'm ready to wait for when I'm needed.'

The driver settled his chin back upon his chest and resumed his munching, but Man could feel his eyes on him as he walked towards the windows.

They were in the window on the left, framed as for a portrait. A naked candle smoked in the centre of their table. Two cups and a dish of what looked to be cold beef lay between them. The rest of the coffee-room, or as much of it as Man could see through the window, was empty.

Pamela Castleton looked young, very young, with the kind

191

of clumsy beauty only the young can possess. It showed through the weariness and grime of her journey and through her shy nervousness at being alone with a man. She kept picking at the plate of meat and dipping and shaking her head, as if she could not yet fully believe in the reality of what she was doing. Man had often seen the same mixture of awe and joy in the faces and gestures of new brides.

Alan Fletcher seemed even more haggard and strengthless than he had that morning at the sitting. The skin of his face sagged in a sickly droop, his cheeks glowed feverishly, his hands moved aimlessly and restlessly through the air. Man thought he looked angry and worried, almost hysterical. He kept glancing guiltily out of the window, and Man had to stand well out of the window's light to keep from being seen.

The watchman stood unmoving in the cold and the dark, not knowing what to do next. He wanted to hear their words, but the glass was thick and set in stone, and he dared not step into the empty coffee-room. He knew that eventually he would go in and confront the ironmonger, but he also felt that the time was not yet right. There was still so much he had to learn. Somehow.

So he waited and he watched.

There was an obvious tension between the two at the table that Man himself gradually came to feel. For an eerie moment, he wondered how the candle flame could continue to burn so steadily in the wash of emotions between the ironmonger and the girl. Alan Fletcher seemed to be accusing the girl of something: he jammed a stiffened finger again and again into the top of the table as if to emphasize his anger. With each prod of the finger, his head jerked forward and his lips strained back. Finally, when Pamela Castleton spread her hands wide in a shrug and arched her body imploringly towards him, the ironmonger rocked back in his chair and looked up at the ceiling with disgust.

Man thought he could understand this part of it well enough. Alan Fletcher had had more troubles than he could bear in the last two days. The girl could not have chosen a worse time to travel all the way from Tilbury to see him. It must have been that which she had written him in the letter, telling him how anxious she was to be with him and arranging this meeting at the coaching-inn. It would have been an unlooked-for complication which the ironmonger could not afford, but which he could not possibly avoid.

But why the girl should have chosen this particular day to come to London, rather than any other, Man could not yet understand. He had no great faith in mere coincidence.

Now Alan Fletcher had begun drinking from a large glass of cloudy gin that had just been brought to the table. For a few long minutes, neither of them spoke. The ironmonger was moody and pouting, a boy who has not been allowed to run out and play. Pamela Castleton sat with her elbows on the table, her trembling hands curled about her mouth. She looked confused and hurt and perhaps for the first time a little frightened.

Man's feet were freezing, and the wind was filling his ears with an icy cold; but he kept his place. He was waiting for something, waiting to see something, although he did not know what.

Suddenly, the ironmonger sat forward and started speaking and gesticulating more energetically than before. He must have been talking to the girl more roughly now, because the watchman could see his words register in the pained shock of her expression. When Alan Fletcher began gesturing impatiently out of the window towards the black night, Man saw the girl's lips repeat the only word he had as yet been able to make out:

the open-mouthed explosion of the shouted word, 'Back!'

Was he sending her back to Tilbury and promising to meet her again at another place, possibly in whichever town he had chosen for his new home? Or was he sending her away? Man could not be sure. But he guessed that Fletcher himself would want to leave the city as soon as he could. The ironmonger had no reason to stay, but he did have many to go. His wife was dead, but the widow, Judith Woodman, was still very much alive; and her greed and suspicion, as well as her close relationships with Zachary Trippuck and Constable Burton, would never let him live in peace. All the cash had been taken from the shop in Green's Alley, and the business itself could be disposed of later from a safe distance. He had to run – out of the city surely, maybe even out of the country. He needed time to let the repercussions of his wife's death settle and be forgotten.

The sympathy that the watchman was now feeling for the girl made him want to rush into the coffee-room at once and steal her away from Alan Fletcher and tell her everything. Yet still Man hesitated. Standing before the lighted window in which the two were acting out their private pantomime, he was reminded of the few plays he had seen at Drury Lane and of his growing excitement as the critical moment of the story approached. There was to be a new play, he suddenly remembered, opening there on Thursday night. Many people were talking about it. *The Lying Lover*.

Man studied the pair in the window more closely. They were posed in silence once again – the ironmonger sipping steadily at his drink and scowling, the girl sitting straight-backed and staring blankly at the waning candle. There was something new in their posture that puzzled the watchman. He felt that he had seen something like it before.

Nicholas and Dorothy Puncheon, proprietors of the shop in

Antelope Alley, had as generally happy a marriage as Man had ever known. He had not seen them fighting often; but when he had, he noticed that they always went about it in the same way. The husband would sit with his back curved into a hump, speaking a few words in a soundless mutter, seemingly ready to look at anything except his wife's face. The tripe-woman would sit with her eyes fixed upon her hands as they pulled at a hanging thread or picked a bit of sausage apart or rubbed a stain in the wood of the table. There would be a tension between them, but it was a bored tension that unmarried lovers never had. They would seem more tired than angry. Nothing that either of them said could be new to the other: they had said and heard it all before.

Alan Fletcher was talking now, but only in short lifeless phrases. His eyes roved from table to chair to window. The girl had made a roof of her hands over her cup and appeared to be seriously cleaning a fingernail. Man could not help it: they looked married to him. And from that thought it was easy to move on to the next – to suppose that they were.

It was a common enough habit among the men of the town. 'Fleet Marriages', they were called – as much for their hurry and shallowness as for the fact that most of them were solemnized in the Fleet Prison chapel. Marriages without benefit of published banns or licence – performed at any time and place and by any man – were by all considered to be perfectly valid, if not properly moral. The precincts of the prisons abounded in opportunities for a man to acquire an extra wife, for a woman to strip her new husband of his fortune before deserting him, or for a rake to lower the defences of a timid maidenhead. The watchman knew a handful of men who had made marrying into a profession; and those who had made it a favourite pastime must have numbered in the thousands.

Now Man saw – because he only now began to look for it –
what he should have seen before: the candlelight glinting off
the girl's left hand as she raised it to her face. A ring.

It was time to move. The watchman quickly scanned the
dark courtyard. There was a boy idling about the nearest stable.
Man whistled him over and handed him a coin.

'The young girl in the coffee-room – there, the pretty one in
the window – is wanted urgently by her driver. Fetch her out at
once, will you? Alone.'

Man followed the boy through the main entrance of the inn.
He stood still in the shadow of a hanging curtain and tried to
slow his breathing. He waited.

Pamela Castleton came out after a minute, walking
uncertainly towards the door. Man stepped forward and gently
cupped her elbow in his hand.

'This way, if you please, Miss.' He spoke with the intangible
authority of the helpful servant.

It was a short walk to the flying-coach, but there was only
one thing that Man wanted to learn from the girl.

'Most sorry, Miss, to take you off so sudden as this. You can
be back in a breath, I promise you.' He could feel her upset
through her arm, and he tried to soften his hold upon her. Their
shoulders brushed together, as he moved closer to her to give
her his support. 'Mighty special day for you, after all, is it not?'

'What?'

Man stopped them just inside the door and tried to speak as
kindly as he could. 'Well, I mean to say, Miss, that I know
you've come in late tonight from Tilbury Town, and you must
be wanting to stay by the gentleman in the coffee-room as long
as you can. It has been some long time – has it not? – since
you've seen your husband all in a piece. And a young lady like
yourself needs that, I know.'

Pamela Castleton was eighteen years old. She may have been worried, distraught, even disillusioned; but she was still a proud and romantic young woman.

The hallway lanthorn was casting its light against the side of Man's face, and it made him look older than he was, and wiser. The girl saw his expression of concern and smiled shyly.

'It is as you say, Sir: we have not been and cannot now be enough together. We have been married the whole of one year this very day, and such anniversaries do mean much to an impressible young girl – though I fear it may mean something less at the time to the man,' she finished, her voice weakening.

The watchman stood silent for a moment, feeling both saddened and angry, then hurried the girl out into the courtyard and towards the flying-coach.

If Raymond Chambers was surprised to see Man walking the girl out of the coaching-inn, he did not show it. In the dark, he seemed to be a wooden projection of the coach itself.

The watchman led Pamela Castleton straight to the side of the coach and unlatched the door.

'But Mr Chambers—'

'The night is cold, Miss, and I doubt not but a frost is promising. You will be safe in here. I'll beg him down to join you.'

She wanted to say something more, but Man hoisted her up and closed and locked the door.

Man talked to the driver for less than a minute, and in that time he told him everything he knew or suspected and what he meant to do. Raymond Chambers said nothing at first, then he sent a bullet of phlegm singing over Man's shoulder and grinned broadly.

'You care for him then, Sir, I trust to you on that. With the wind fallen as it has, I can see no stoppage for us 'twixt here and Tilbury. The horses is rested enough.'

Man barely had time to climb down before the whip snapped and the wheels of the coach lumbered into motion. The girl's muffled shouting receded across the empty courtyard.

Alan Fletcher still had the coffee-room to himself. The candle on his table was the only light, and the room was filled with sombre unmoving shadows. The ironmonger was staring moodily out of the window, and Man was able to drop into the girl's chair before the other had noticed him.

Man gave him no time at all.

'You should not, Mr Fletcher, have replaced the bloodied spade quite so neatly among the others. What other person save yourself would have done that?'

The ironmonger stared stupidly at Man, as if he had just been given advice in a foreign language.

'Do what?' he muttered thickly.

'The spade, Sir,' Man went on evenly, quietly. 'A man – or a woman even – strikes and kills another savagely in hatred and in madness. When he is done with his work, he throws the weapon thoughtlessly aside, or he forgets and carries it abroad with him. He does not carefully return it to its rightful place – unless he is in his own home, where his wife has bothered him so for years past with the arranging of their possessions in a proper order. It is a habit, Sir, that cannot be erased in a single night. It is done as it is done every day – without thought.'

Alan Fletcher gasped and his face turned whiter. A nervous smacking started up in his mouth, a wet sucking of the back of the tongue against the palate that persisted throughout the rest of the conversation. It did not seem to bother Man in the slightest.

There was something deeply unsettling about the watchman's easy composure. He slowly brought his pipe out of his pocket, filled it leisurely, and set it burning with the candle. He did not clamp the stem tightly between his teeth, as a man will when he is working hard, but instead held it loosely cradled in the palm of his hand. He might have been talking to an old and trusted friend about past troubles in the family.

The ironmonger struggled against his panic by assuming a fragile indignation.

'If you have been listening of late, Sir, to the hateful insinuations of Madam Woodman—'

Man spread his hands. 'Not at all, Sir. I have merely come to know you in a very small time; and I know that it may be possible for a man to change what he does – often suddenly and violently – but he cannot change what he is. And you, Sir, are much a man of fixed habits, both by day and by night.'

A scuffling of footsteps reached them from the corridor, and the ironmonger stiffened in alarm. Man gestured casually towards the invisible courtyard.

'No need to worry yourself upon that matter, Sir. I have just this moment sent Miss Castleton flying back to her home in Tilbury. I trust that her father will take her into his house again and that she will have learned something needful from what she has lately suffered.' Man's tone became bitter. 'She is still very young, is she not, Mr Fletcher?'

The ironmonger looked offended. 'She is a woman, Sir – now.'

Man drew his pipe from his mouth, his lips puckering, as if the taste of the smoke had suddenly turned sour. He laid the pipe upon the table and kept looking at it as he spoke.

'And that's to be set to your account, Sir, if I understand the situation aright. A young girl has but one mark of her youth and innocence; and when that is taken from her – stolen from her – she is carried into womanhood whether she be ready for it or no.' The watchman came face to face with Alan Fletcher.

'The letter she wrote you yesterday from Tilbury must have frightened you much, Sir.'

Man had said it quietly and without emphasis, as if he were merely reporting a recognized fact. The ironmonger might have made any answer, or none at all; but in his nervousness and surprise he gave the worst response he could have given.

'You found it?'

'I did, Sir,' Man said evenly, but at the same time he quickly picked up his pipe and busied himself with refilling it. 'And a sorry document it is. Would you care to read it over once again?' He slowly moved his hand into an empty pocket of his greatcoat.

The ironmonger shook his head and gulped down the last of his gin.

'I have a cousin named Charles,' the watchman went on conversationally, 'whose wife is likewise affected overmuch by the coming on of every anniversary. Women will be so, though, will they not? They will not stay to count the inconvenience.'

Alan Fletcher retreated into a stubborn silence, but at the same time he began to shake slightly in his limbs and jowls. He looked about the room – first moving only his eyes, then his head – as if he were searching for a way to escape. The nervous smacking in his mouth grew louder and more regular, as an old woman will click her tongue when she is becoming frustrated over a stitch.

The two men did not speak for a long while. Outside, a coach drew up and spilled out its passengers. Horses and men stamped their feet in the cold, and women's voices were raised against the servants as they heard their trunks being hurled to the ground. The coaching-inn hurried into motion to welcome the new guests in.

Inside the coffee-room, the men sat together by the window, waiting.

Man spoke first.

'I am much surprised, Sir, that you should think to take Miss Castleton to wife. With the failing of Mr Defoe's brickworks, her father cannot have so much that you could hope to gain by the union.'

'If you will allow me, Sir . . .' the ironmonger said and rose unsteadily to his feet. His thigh pushed against the edge of the table as he moved to leave.

'What, then, is to keep you, Mr Fletcher, these few years hence from taking the selfsame spade to Pamela Castleton as well?'

Alan Fletcher stopped and frowned down at the watchman.

'She is different.'

'How?'

The line of his lips tightened. 'She is mine, Sir.'

'As was one named Joan Parker.'

'No, never,' the ironmonger muttered, staring down at the outline of his fingertips against the discoloured wood of the table. 'Not even at the starting.'

'And so you killed her.'

A slight smile accompanied by a click of the tongue.

'Have I admitted it, Sir?'

'You have not had cause to do so – yet. When the time comes, I am certain that Mr Trippuck will tell the magistrate as much as will need be known. For now, sit you down again, Sirrah.' Man sighed wearily with just a hint of a threat. 'There is nowhere you can run to.'

Fletcher had smiled more broadly at the mention of his friend's name, but he meekly took to his chair again and sat with his short arms crossed upon the table. There was a single dark stain at the end of the right sleeve, but the watchman did not seem to notice it.

'I am myself as yet unmarried,' Man continued with visible embarrassment, 'and I have as well no great knowledge of any woman. And I never had the chance to know your wife, Sir, during her life, although I have heard some words about her since her death.' He paused. 'But why, I wonder, did you care to choose as your life's partner one of the workers at Madam Betty's Cock and Bull? You surely knew of her past.'

The ironmonger seemed surprised at Man's knowing so much. He carefully studied the watchman's face, then looked down at the table and began to pick away at a loosened sliver of wood.

'I did not choose, Sir; I was chosen.'

'No man lets himself be used in any way which lies against him.'

'Have you said "no man", Sir?' Alan Fletcher said the words with an unnatural calmness. 'If you mean to call me "boy", pray do not feel obliged to use any other term.'

'You are a boy, then,' the watchman replied easily.

In an instant, the ironmonger's face was transformed as though by the jerk of a muscle. The upper lip curled at one side, deep grooves appeared around the mouth, and the scalp twitched. Even the eyes seemed somehow different in colour and shape.

'Boy or man, Sir, there are some things which no one has the power to resist!'

'Which things are those, then?'

Fletcher stared vacantly before him, not seeing the watchman, reliving the past.

'They are trained to please – the girls at the Cock and Bull – trained very well. And their method is to please by shamming a pleasure of their own. They can make a man feel – more a man with their coarse words and their noises and their moving. A man knows that there have been others – so many others – but he is made to feel that he is the first to bring forth that particular moan, that one sudden sigh. She gasps and screams and begs him never to stop – and all the while her eye is trained upon the clock on the opposite wall. Can you not understand, Sir? Each man is led to think himself unique, special, the only one to . . . And there are scores of them – hundreds, thousands – and to the woman each one has been the same. To them it is a trade as mine is iron – nothing more. Yet to each one of the men it is a dream, a dream. The slapping of their thighs together –' his voice became cringing, pathetic '– I swear to you it echoes in his ears precisely like applause.'

The watchman spoke with a deep revulsion which the other did not hear.

'Yet if you were not her first, Sir, you were her last. She became your wife.'

'And gained a name and a good shop by the move, Sir! And takes the running of the iron as if it were her own to take. And what remains to me? To be a speechless servant within my own house – and with nothing but abuse for wages! To wonder at every chapman that gains the door – he who comes for nails may once have been the very one who stroked the inside of her thigh, the fat man after harness may have covered her oftener than I, the one who takes up the spade—' He broke off as he saw Man watching him more closely. 'No matter, it is the same. You cannot know, Sir, what it is to see yourself in every man, to find the marks of your own secret pleasures in another man's eyes. I have turned more than one out the door as empty-handed as he came for the merest suggestion of a smile in her presence.'

'Yet you have these years returned yourself nightly to the riot of the Cock and Bull at a cost to your name and your pocket. Now I must ask you why, Sir. Why choose to run the same road over and again? Do the other girls differ so greatly from one another or from your wife?'

Here the ironmonger seemed almost joyful in his eagerness to explain.

'Not at all, Sir, not at all. They are each one but more and more of the same. It is I – I myself – who have been changed! I know the tricks of their play now, and I can take them as they deserve to be taken – quickly and with a drunken, forgetful roar. I know they do not care who it is that mounts them, and knowing it helps me to ride them all the harder. And let me tell you something more, Sir,' Fletcher continued, aiming a quivering finger at Man's chest, 'something that no mere "boy" could ever guess at. Each loud night that I spent sporting at the hummum did but arm me the better for the following day, when I could keep the shop beside my loving dame and know inside that I had done her own deed back at her and done it one better. Why, I might have kept a tally of it on the wall to prove to her how every sweating night kept me another mark ahead of her! Whatever she may have done earlier, I did later – and worse!'

'What was your marriage, then,' the watchman mused, 'but one long and repeating vengeance?'

The other man sat back with a condescending smirk. 'What else is there, Sir, between a man and a woman, but the crying constant need for making even?'

Young George Man was looking at the ironmonger with the disbelieving wonder of one who encounters a new species of creature whose strange habits he simply cannot understand.

'To pay your night-time revels,' Man went on after a short pause, 'must have had you turning and winding each penny in your hand – hence the dark trade with Alex Woodman and that in bricks and tiles with Mr Defoe. A man's pleasures come dear, and I cannot imagine your late wife ever lending you the coin to keep you in them.'

'Mrs Fletcher,' the other replied sourly, 'was used to be as cautious with our moneys as you are, Sir, with your man's yard. If she'd a third hand, it'd have been as hard-closed as the other two. I never glimpsed so much as the edge of any coin that entered the house. Can you think what it is, Sir, for a man to have to plead for the ready to supply him with his morning cup of ale? Her trade, remember, had also been in the taking of money for dulling labour; and the shop merely gave her the means to earn it for once upon her feet. My wife, Sir, slid herself beneath my shop as another woman would beneath her lover. Even in our bed, those few times that she remained awake long enough, I fancied I could hear the hidden tinkling of guineas under my hand.'

'Perhaps she was only anxious for a security which she had never known. Her family, I understand, came from a low, dark street.'

Alan Fletcher made no reply to this, but only stared moodily down into his empty glass and then towards the coffee-room door, as if he were hoping for the sudden appearance of a bar-boy. His plump face looked haggard, and his nervous lips were wet and pouting.

Man continued pressing him. 'I have this day talked long with Judith Woodman. Her deep silence must have cost you much, Sir.'

'And there's t'other of the pair! Between them they made as hard a pair of pincers as was ever wrought!'

'The widow knew all? Of your repeated visits, I mean to say, to Madam Betty's bagnio?'

'She knew enough to hold the threat of my good wife's ire against my frolics and to make me pay.'

'And for the death of Mr Woodman as well?'

The ironmonger went on as though he had not heard. 'If you should wish to know something true of woman, Sir, I can tell you this: they will never, never see themselves in error! The fault is forever ours, and they will show it you before you can see it yourself. What is nature in them is called viciousness in us. My wife no sooner saw the walls of the Cock and Bull behind her than she set herself to lecturing me on the sins of whoring. She! And the widow working to bleed a man of his play, while all the while she and Zachary . . .' His look became sly, oily. 'But that, too, has now been put aright – to my satisfaction!'

A bustle of feet and voices was growing in the hall. The night-time activities of the coaching-inn were beginning; supper would be laid soon. The coffee-room was still an island of quiet – cold, immobile, a vacuum – but the moving noises seemed to be coming nearer the door at every pass. At any moment, the door might be opened by a harried servant bringing in fresh lights, trays of steaming food, lively and joking people.

The watchman sat crouched wearily over the table, his left hand slowly massaging his forehead while his right sketched invisible designs across the wood. He might have been tabulating a column of figures or dating and arranging a series of actions.

Alan Fletcher was restless, but waiting almost patiently. At irregular intervals he would make the snicking noise with his tongue, and the sound had the maddening persistence of dripping water.

Man spoke softly from behind his raised arm.

'With the waning of Mr Defoe's business, your private purse was gone.'

The ironmonger made no sound.

'And yet Robin must continue to be pleased.'

The ironmonger shifted his feet.

'And the widow must still be paid.'

A wet smack of the mouth.

'And then the letter from the young girl, demanding to be reunited once and away with the secret husband she has not seen for so long. And then comes the useful cover and distraction of the storm.'

Fletcher made a low gagging noise in his throat.

'And Judith Woodman, because she is in the house, may be conveniently charged with the deed. And then her demands for more payment would be stopped.'

The ironmonger started to speak, but Man suddenly brought his head up and broke out in loud anger, his shoulders hunched up almost to his ears.

'All this, Sir, all this I can understand. I can trace the course of it well enough; I can even see the need for what you were moved to do, though I shall never concede its justness. You had, to your mind, little other remedy: doing nothing had been made impossible, and you were bound to move in the direction in which your nature moved you. This all, I say, is clear enough. The coming together of a man and a woman – a marriage – must be, I should think, the most difficult and proving work on earth, second only perhaps to the bringing of a child to age. No person is perfect; no two can ever think or feel or like in precisely the same way. There are differing fears and jealousies, peculiar hatreds and sufferings that will always act between them to confuse and estrange them one from the other. They must be together, yet they cannot *be* each other. It is a problem that can never be forgotten – and never wholly resolved.' The watchman leaned forward with his fists pressing into the table. 'But what I cannot understand is why – in the name of Christ's blood, man – why you should have felt yourself obliged to carry the poor girl into all this. She is young and simple and trusting, but she may be so no longer – and that is your work. If there be crime here, it is this. Your wife is dead, and her hope must lie hereafter between herself and God. But Pamela Castleton's life lies before her still, though she may now wish it did not.' Man reached across the table and gripped Fletcher's smooth wrist hard. 'Can the easy winning of a maidenhead really mean so very much to you, Sirrah?'

The ironmonger looked down at the dark hand covering his, then up. A fine film of white spittle clung to his lips.

'No, no, no. You understand nothing, Sir. Nothing.'

'Then tell me why!'

'To be seen for once, Sir,' he answered quietly, simply. 'Only to be seen. Not to be looked round and over and through, as though I were nothing above a discounted scrap of dead iron or a noisome little boy who is only to be suffered. To be special to someone for the first time, and not to be made to feel so much alone.'

After a long and silent minute, the watchman's hand slowly drew back.

On the long walk back to Westminster, neither man spoke a word. The watchman seemed worn and troubled, and Alan Fletcher moved in a numb trance. At one point a hawker shouted his wares into his face – 'Hot baked wardens and pippins, Sir!' – but he only smiled stupidly and pushed past.

As they walked by St Paul's, they passed through the fringes of a group of laughing men and yelling boys. In the centre stood the waterman, Henry Dow, upending still another leather bottle and telling for the hundredth time how he had waked this morning at the Tower Dock, feeling perfectly safe and rested. As he told it, he could not stop shaking his head.

Chapter 5

In the Parish of Capal by Darking lived one Charles
Man, who was in bed with his wife and two children, and
by a fall of part of his house, he and one child were
killed, and his wife, and the other child, miraculously
preserved . . .

By Thursday, the ninth day of December, the citizens of
Westminster and London had learned enough of the facts of the
storm and its effects to keep them remembering and talking at
least through the following year. Reported numbers and places
may have varied slightly from street to street, but the general
picture was clear. And though some of the older men argued
that this had been nothing compared to that in 1661 – 18
February, a dark Tuesday, when the fish had been blown out of
the water in the Park, birds beaten out of flight, and the heads
had been plucked off the spikes at Westminster Hall and rolled
thumping through the streets – they were soon shouted down
with new stories or new inventions. All agreed that they prayed
never to feel such a wind again.

In London alone, two thousand chimneys had been downed;
in St James's Park, one hundred strong elms. Two hundred
people lay injured, many of them given up for dead. Very few
houses had escaped undamaged, and most of the streets still

had piles of unsalvageable debris standing at their sides.

In the country, countless cocks of hay had been blown apart, ricks of corn had been heaved in a body off the staddle. Thousands of thatched roofs had disappeared: the price of reed rose at once from twenty shillings to fifty, and the poor had to make do with bean, helm, or furze. Nearly twenty thousand trees covered the fields of Kent, and at Huntspill a crowd of ships stood awkwardly upon dry land.

Eight thousand men were lost at sea, two thousand of them naval men. And the Queen was said to be contemplating supporting their relatives out of the public funds.

Total dead on land were figured at one hundred and twenty-five or -three, depending upon whether or not the deaths of Joan Fletcher and Zachary Trippuck were regarded as storm-related.

On the afternoon of that Thursday, George Man was standing in front of an apothecary's shop in Jermyn Street near the Park. The proprietor, Josepp Clench, was showing him the newly-repaired roof and telling him how the two stacks of chimneys of five funnels each had been flung through the roof and on to the upstairs bed where his only child had been sleeping with a servant. His voice still shook with relief as he described how quickly the two girls' bruises and cuts had healed.

Man turned to take a closer look at the apothecary. He saw a healthy man with a broad, clear face whose natural hair stood up in thin wisps like a cock's blade. Josepp Clench seemed to be an especially gentle man with the straightforward, kind manner of a good midwife. Man guessed it was this, as much as his medical skills, that had persuaded Charles Dickinson to transfer Isabella Trippuck to a vacant room in Clench's house. Her physical injuries had mended well, but she still kept to her bed and dozed fitfully throughout the day.

Josepp Clench led the watchman through a neat shop that smelled of wood and herbs and upstairs to a small bedroom at the front. On the way, Man glimpsed a tiny eye – blackened, but smiling – winking shyly at him from around a corner.

The woman was sitting up in bed, her tired eyes fixed upon the lighted square of window. The sharp winter sunlight brought out all the lines in her face and made her look older, although Man could not be sure of this: he had never before seen her by day.

The watchman introduced himself with a formal bow and a few hurried words of explanation. He felt as he always did in the presence of suffering, uneasy and uncomprehending.

For as long as his conversation with Isabella Trippuck lasted, Man had to struggle against the disquieting sensation that the woman knew exactly what he was going to say before he said it – almost, it seemed, before he himself knew.

'I must offer you, Madam, my sincerest condolences upon the late death of your husband. I did not know him at all myself, but I think no man deserves such an unlooked-for ending.'

'He was a man, I fear, like any other,' Isabella Trippuck answered in a low voice, 'something far from perfection. He ran too often shouting through the streets, to his pain and mine; but it is enough that I remember those times when I have heard him whisper.' She gazed sightlessly towards the window for a time, turned back to the watchman and gestured wearily with her hand. 'But prithee seat yourself, Sir. There is no use to your standing.'

Man pulled over a heavy elbow-chair and sat down. He felt himself sitting straighter than usual, and he found that he could not always meet the woman's eyes.

'I trust, Madam, that it will be some satisfaction to you to know that the man who killed your husband will be himself driven to Tyburn before the year is done with the deaths of two lying upon his soul.'

'I think it will be none at all to me, Sir.' The hollowness of her voice made the watchman squirm.

After a silence Man said, 'It appears he was moved – this man, Alan Fletcher – to his actions partly by the continued extorting of moneys from him by the widow of Alex Woodman. She is fated, I think, to pass her Christmas in Bridewell, beating at the hemp and praying good Sir Robert to knock.' Constable Burton, Man knew, had already found himself another mistress.

The woman in bed accepted this information with no change of expression and no reply.

'You yourself, Madam, paid much to her these past three years, did you not?'

Her calm eyes widened. 'I needed much.'

'There are other lenders enough in the town – a few, no doubt, asking slightly less increase at the return.'

Man now saw Isabella Trippuck hesitate a bit, as if his words had put her on her guard.

'The lady's husband had been cruelly taken from her,' she answered carefully. 'I pitied her.'

The watchman sat quiet for a while, listening to the muted noises from the street and feeling the warmth of the yellow light that suffused the room. He knew what he had to say next, and he wished there were an easier way to say it.

'The killing of Alex Woodman, then. A mean blow, that; a most wicked assassination. The men that sullied their hands in that had nothing to take pride in.' Man paused and watched her eyes closely. 'Nor their womenkind neither, if they had knowledge of it.'

He saw it: a shocked fluttering of the eyelids.

'A feeling woman,' he hurried on, 'might take the part of

212

another woman even before her own husband. That is not impossible. Yet she might also wish to secure her husband from harm and protect him from those who knew the truth. She might even continue to trade at the shop of a rival, if only to keep herself and him in the other's good graces. It is no surprise: 'twas a shop that dealt in silence to any who needed it.'

Isabella Trippuck said nothing, but to Man her growing restlessness was confirmation enough. He wondered how much she knew of the true relationship between the widow and her husband. Man thought that he knew Judith Woodman better: to have lain beneath the hands of her husband's murderer must have been for the widow a new and strange excitement.

The watchman suddenly changed his tone and began to talk idly of the storm and of the city's efforts to return to normal life. He stood up and strode over to the window, speaking casually of some of the many things he had witnessed during the last week. He reached out to touch the warm glass.

'The storm itself drew many matters to a head. I think, Madam, that we could see then the best and the worst in us: the courage and endurance we never knew was ours, as well as the fears and weaknesses which ought never to be discovered. 'Tis these last that wound the deepest: the suspicion, the anger, the jealousy.' Man turned from the window. 'A jealous man may do anything, may he not, Madam? Even what is unconceivable ...'

When he saw the woman's legs jerk reflexively together underneath the bed-clothes, Man knew he had guessed right. Isabella Trippuck had been attacked and violated by three men, one of whom was her own husband.

'And will you grieve for him still, Madam?' the watchman asked when he reached the door.

She looked up at him in plain surprise.

'He was my husband, Sir; I was his wife.'

Not understanding, Man bowed silently and left the room.

The evening of that same Thursday was the second time in a week that George Man deliberately failed to report himself for the watch.

The first had been last Thursday night, when he had attended the opening of *The Lying Lover*. It was a comedy, preposterous and light, and the audience had received it well. For some reason, Man had sat through the entire programme without a smile.

Tonight he stood within a small circle of people in front of a dingy coal shop at the north-east corner of Jerusalem Passage. The house belonged to one Thomas Britton, a perpetually sooty and cheerful man of about fifty years of age. He was a small-coal man who daily went about his business with as much dogged joy as if he were delivering gifts of cash to the poor. He never missed a day's work; and every Thursday night he opened the top storey of his house for a pleasant entertainment of fine music, provided free of charge to all. And he had been doing the same for the past quarter of a century.

In the street with Man stood the entire household of Michael Wells and Elizabeth Man, the watchman's mother. Tetty Man had never missed one of Britton's concerts yet: she had even come the week in 1695 when her husband, Samuel, had died. Never more than now, she had said, had she needed the clear comfort of an evening of soothing music.

Michael Wells was in high spirits. The wind had brought him more orders than he could meet, and now he kept insisting loudly that they all retire to the nearest tavern for a last quartern or two. His wife was shushing him with all the patient practice of ages. The son, Daniel Wells, kept shaking his head in youthful embarrassment for his father.

Sarah stood apart – quiet, content, self-possessed.

A hackney-coach had been called to take Tetty Man back to Old Street. Man stood beside it now, directing the driver to put up the tin-sashes perforated with small holes that served as windows. The night was clear, but cold, and there was a fresh wind.

The watchman turned to look at his mother. The light from the thick convex lamp at the end of the street showed him her full-blown cheeks, the yeasty texture of fresh ale. She was smiling at him and clicking her tongue.

'You are to take greater care for yourself in the future, George. Why, marry, last week it was your face put me in mind of a Good Friday bun, what with the cuts on it and all, and it still lies a long yard from clearing.'

Man looked at his mother with patient affection.

'I take as great care as I can, Madam. 'Tis a roaring town.'

She started to say something more, but the watchman dutifully kissed her on the forehead and briskly handed her up into the coach.

In a few minutes the small group was moving leisurely down St John's Street. The crowds were thick and loud, and by the time they reached Fleet Market they were forced to wedge themselves through a churning confusion of dickering shoppers and cries of 'Come buy my fine cucumbers to pickle!' It seemed as if most of the town had taken to the streets to savour the clear night and the refreshing wind.

It took all Man's most expert manoeuvring, but eventually he was able to separate himself and Sarah from the rest of the family. Michael Wells noticed their hanging back at once, and he turned with a bantering voice to caution the youngsters against playing at hoop-and-hide behind his back. His wife turned his head forward again with a light slap, and he set himself to whistling the tune of 'Now Ponder Well, You Parents Dear'.

The watchman walked as closely beside the young woman as he dared.

'I can tell you now, Mistress Wells, that the man who made so bold as to affront you this week last before the Royal Cockpit did soon after meet his death by violent means. He was a man of the most vicious habits.'

Sarah Wells walked on with her eyes on the road at her feet.

'Nay, I will take no pleasure,' she finally responded, 'in the unhappy death of any man.'

'Yet he was one that ran towards his the whole of his life.'

'What was his name, do you know?'

'Zachary Trippuck, a sometime sack-weaver at Woolstaple Market.'

'Did he have a wife and children?' she asked slowly.

'No children, but – yes, he left his wife.' There was a note of deep uncertainty in the watchman's voice.

'I grieve for her then in her sorrow. Who was it that killed him?'

They followed the signpainter and his wife and son out of Fleet Market and into the bright bustle of Fleet Street.

'An ironmonger it was from Green's Alley, one by the name of Alan Fletcher. He stabbed him most foully the day after the storm – having, the night before, murdered as well his own wife.' Man's voice began to fail him at the end, as if he were reluctant to tell her too much.

'Why?'

The simplicity of the question disconcerted the watchman. He waited a long while to answer.

'Because of hatred, Mistress Wells – a hatred born of a great hurting, neither of which I can now pretend to understand.'

It was nearing ten o'clock as they came in front of St Dunstan's, and Michael Wells insisted upon their joining the crowd that had gathered to watch the two wooden savages strike the hour. Man knew that the city's pickpockets congregated here to work the gawking spectators, and he was instantly on his guard.

As the figures struck the bell and the crowd murmured, the watchman noticed a bent and shrivelled man moving too close to the side of the young woman. Man stepped over and laid his hand firmly upon the withered shoulder.

'Nay, not at this stall, Kay. There's safer pockets for you over the street.'

The crippled man gave a start, felt the weight of the hand at his shoulder, and scurried off.

When they were moving again, Sarah Wells asked, 'And do you think, Sir, to keep yourself long in the parish watch? That would be quite uncommon in a gentleman of your young age, would it not?'

Man started speaking before the woman had finished. 'No, I think not. That is, the watch has so little to promise a man for his future.' He hesitated and turned to study her profile in the half-light. 'Yet I cannot say for certain at this time. There is something in the work – I do not know what – which holds me to it.'

'Mayhap it is the people's need that calls you.'

'The innocent, yes.' Man nodded. 'They want the safe-keeping.'

Sarah Wells almost broke her stride and her voice grew stronger. 'Nay, the guilty, Sir. They need the watching more. The angered, the hungered, the maddened and the wild – any of those who strive to forget for the moment the pain of being a man.'

They were coming up to Charing Cross when the watchman spoke again.

'I must tell you, then, that I have had of late a very kind proposal from a gentleman to enter myself into his house with him. I think the trade would please me, and I know my mother would feel more kindly towards it. She is forever holding forth upon the wisdom of a cousin of mine near Darking who is well-set in the calendering line and whose future, she swears, is secure.'

'Is it the Royal Coffee-House you speak of, Sir?' Sarah Wells said, straining her neck to see farther down the street. 'The proprietor of that is of your family as well, is he not?'

She had named one of the most fashionable shops in the city, and Man's face grew warm in the frozen air as he quickly explained that Alexander Man was no relation.

'Yet you ought not to concern yourself, Sir, too much with what is said of your work. You may yourself bring honour to it.' Her voice became kinder, slightly less formal. 'And that will prove enough for you – and your wife – provided you select a match of simple prudence and common good liking.'

Man knew the Wells family would soon be turning off King Street and towards the Park: he had no time to lose.

'Of that,' he said very seriously, 'I should like to speak with you again in some detail.'

Sarah Wells turned then and smiled.

'It is not in me, Sir; you must come home and ask my father.'

A high-pitched shouting suddenly overtook them from behind. A small boy raced past, trailing behind him a string that rose and disappeared into the dark air towards the invisible kite that the wind was sailing somewhere far overhead.

Man could not see it, did not look for it. He was watching the peaceful face of the young woman, Sarah Wells.